2

Mark Allan Gunnells

Valhalla Books
www.valhallabooks.com

2B

Valhalla Books Publisher

www.valhallabooks.com

ISBN: 9798573555683

Dedication

To Karen Gainey and Warren Rochelle, two college professors who took me seriously in my youth and made me feel like a real writer.
-Mark Allan Gunnells

***

"When your ex wants you dead, they will take you to the grave with them!" -2 B

As a small print publisher, I thoroughly enjoy working with Mark Allan Gunnells. He is a compelling storyteller who fleshes out characters for what he likes to call a "slow burn." I enjoy reading his work and am excited to publish *2B:*

Adam Messer

Publisher

Valhalla Books

Hall of Honor

Thank you to our Patreon Supporters!

James Burns – Viking of Valhalla

Dennis Crawford – Champion of Valhalla

Michelle Cornwell-Jordan – Guardian of Valhalla

Darrell Grizzle – Guardian of Valhalla

To support future Valhalla Books projects and have your name listed in the Hall of Honor:
http://www.patreon.com/adammesser

There you are my friend! We finally found you!
Lo though we journey through dark lands filled with horrors of the night, we go not alone. Pick up yer gear and join us as we travel across time and space.
For Valhalla Books! - **Lars Krieger**
https://mailchi.mp/797031433c49/valhalla-books

1: Discharge

Berkley Simmons couldn't wait to go home.

Actually, that wasn't entirely true. He couldn't wait to get out of the hospital, with its lime green walls and stench of disinfectant barely covering the smell of sickness and decay, but the idea of returning to his apartment filled him with dread. If he had anywhere else to go ... well, if wishes were horses and all that jazz.

He could get a motel room somewhere, but money was tight enough and the paltry health insurance provided by his job at the bookstore would still leave him deeply in debt from this little three day vacation at Spartanburg Regional.

If he asked, Sasha would probably let him crash at her place, but her live-in mooch of a boyfriend Jeffrey hated Berkley. Probably because Berkley didn't really hide the fact that he thought Jeffrey was leeching off Sasha. The two had never officially "moved in together." Jeffrey had simply started staying over until he became a permanent fixture like the abstract paintings Sasha hung on her walls.

Berkley's only real family was his older brother Zachary, but the two hadn't spoken since their mother passed away three years ago. Not even an exchange of cards on birthdays and holidays. Hell, they weren't even linked on any social media platforms.

So that left Berkley with nowhere to go but home. The old saying went home was the place that when you had to go there, they had to take you. However, he had always wanted to amend it to, "Home is the place that you have to go to, even when you'd rather go anywhere else."

"Are you okay?" Sasha asked. She sat in a cushioned chair the same putrid color as the walls while Berkley paced around the small hospital room.

"I'm fine. They wouldn't be releasing me today if I wasn't fine. Why wouldn't I be fine?"

"Oh, I don't know. You just seem a little … tense."

Berkley forced himself to stop pacing and took a seat on the edge of the bed. The bed he'd woken up in three days ago, after having nearly been killed.

Correction, you were *killed. If not for Ernie, you'd be in a box underground at the Greenlawn Cemetery right now.*

"Of course I'm tense. After everything that happened, how else should I feel?"

Sasha shrugged with one shoulder, a trademark move of hers. "Maybe grateful to be alive."

"It's hard to feel alive in this hospital. It's like being in hell."

Berkley had never liked hospitals, not since his father had died in one when Berkley was only twelve years old. The family (Berkley, Zachary, and their mother) had visited his dad in the cancer ward of this very hospital, and Berkley had barely recognized the man. His father had always been strong and stout, but the Halloween creature wasting in the bed had been a skeleton wrapped in burlap, eyes bulging out like those creepy stress balls, hair colorless and brittle as straw. Even though Berkley had been old enough to realize it was the cancer eating away at his father, in a weird way he had held the hospital responsible. As if the very environment had caused his rapid decline to oblivion.

Even now, Berkley could hear the alien beeping and whirring of machinery monitoring vitals and helping people breath. Simply being here made his skin itch as if he'd been exposed to poison ivy. He could feel the combined weight of all the disease and desperation housed in this place weighing down on him.

"You look like you want to punch someone," Sasha said, glancing down at Berkley's lap.

He followed her gaze to see he was reflexively balling his hands into fists then relaxing them. "I'd like to punch that damn nurse right in her smug face."

"Janice? She seemed perfectly lovely."

"Yeah, well, she won't let me leave. Treating me like I'm a cripple or something."

"It's hospital policy," Sasha said. "Someone has to wheel you down to the lobby after discharge. Think of it as a free ride."

"She said someone would be by an hour ago, and we're still waiting."

Sasha looked at her cell phone screen. "It has only been ten minutes."

"That's still ten minutes longer than I should have to be here."

Standing, Sasha crossed the room and settled next to Berkley on the bed. Leaning to the side, she bumped his shoulder with her own. "I'm not going to pretend I know what you're going through, so if you need to rant and rave, by all means have at it. However, I do want you to know that I'm here for you."

Berkley felt a sharp retort rise in his throat like bile, but when he looked at his friend and saw nothing but sincerity in her eyes, he swallowed the words and took a deep breath. "I know I'm being a royal pain in the ass. I'm sorry."

"Honey, you don't have to apologize. Considering everything that has happened, I'd say you're dealing remarkably well. Better than I would be. You know me, I'd be an emotional wreck."

Berkley forced a laugh. He couldn't honestly say he wasn't feeling like a wreck, but emotional? There was his distaste for the hospital, the underlying dread of returning to his apartment (*the scene of the crime*, as it were), but beyond that … nothing. A numbness, emotional paralysis if such a thing existed. Dr. Mirza – the ER doc who had taken care of Berkley, monitoring him and making sure he didn't develop pneumonia from the fluid that had filled his lungs – had said this was common among people who had suffered trauma, assuring him the emotional detachment would fade over time.

Berkley wasn't sure that came off as comforting as Mirza had hoped, feeling more like a threat than a reassurance. Whatever emotions Berkley's psyche kept at bay, did he really want to experience them, all crashing over him at once? Perhaps it was safer here in this cocoon of non-feeling.

He abruptly stood and began pacing again, feeling oddly wired as if he'd drank a dozen cups of coffee. Sitting still made the itchy feeling worse. "I think they forgot about me. I'll bet that idiot nurse didn't even tell anyone to come get me. We should leave, screw waiting for a wheelchair that I don't even need. I mean, what are they going to do if I go downstairs on foot, call the cops?"

"No need to make a break for it," Sasha said, rising from the bed herself. "Here comes your chariot."

Berkley glanced through the door and saw an orderly wheeling the chair toward the room, though not a traditional wheelchair. This was a bulky thing with a padded seat and an open cart to store belongings. Kind of like a non-motorized version of those scooters old people drove around in grocery stores. Was this policy really designed for the comfort and convenience of departing patients, or merely a way to humiliate them on their way out the door?

"Train pulling into the station," the orderly said as he stopped just outside the door. He was young, thick dark hair disheveled in a stylish way, full lips spread in a bright smile. The type of guy Berkley would have found irresistibly attractive under other circumstances. Now he noted the man's good looks with a dispassionate disinterest, as if admiring a nice piece of furniture. You could appreciate a Regency style table, but you didn't want to make out with it.

Without acknowledging the orderly's lame joke, Berkley climbed onto the contraption. "Let's go."

"Don't you want to take this?" Sasha asked, picking up a little stuffed bunny from the table by the room's window.

Berkley smirked. "What am I, five? I outgrew stuffed animals a long time ago. Chuck it in the trash."

Sasha hesitated. "Yeah, but this is from Ernie. I thought you might want to keep it for sentimental reasons since, well, you know."

Berkley stared at her in silence for half a minute then craned his neck to look back at the orderly. "Get me the hell out of here."

The young man's smile faltered then reasserted itself. "You got it. All aboard, next stop is the lobby."

*

Sasha backed into a space in front of Berkley's building and cut the engine. She made no move to get out of the car, seemingly content to take her cue from Berkley. He did not move either. He glanced to his right, seeing his rusted Honda in its usual spot where it had sat for the three days he'd been gone like a faithful dog waiting for its master to return from a trip. He then turned his gaze to the apartment building.

Not that there was much to see. Industrial gray siding, a perfectly square structure that Berkley mused resembled a giant cracker box, filled with animal crackers shaped like people. Of course, people were nothing more than animals once you stripped away all the trappings of civilization and civility. The building contained four identical apartments, two downstairs and two upstairs. Berkley's apartment was upstairs on the right.

Sasha held her silence for a full five minutes then placed a gentle hand on Berkley's shoulder. "Wanna come have a sleepover at my place tonight?"

"I doubt Jeffrey would want me underfoot."

"Jeffrey wouldn't mind," Sasha said, but she had always been a terrible liar. Her obvious tell was the way she cut her eyes downward as she tucked a nonexistent stray hair behind her ear. "In fact, he would have come with me to pick you up from the hospital, only he couldn't get out of work."

Berkley nodded but thought, *He stocks shelves at Walmart. How hard could it have been to get the time off?*

"Better if I get it over with," Berkley said. "You know, rip the Band-Aid right off in one quick motion. I mean, I can't exactly afford to move right now, so I'm going to have to get used to staying here."

Sasha looked as if she had something more to say on the subject, but before she could Berkley popped open the door and stepped out onto the cracked pavement. She followed suit. Scanning the small lot, Berkley saw no sign of Ernie's Jeep Grand Cherokee and breathed a sigh of relief. His neighbor was nice enough, and Berkley certainly owed the man a great debt, but he didn't have the energy right now for a long conversation. And Ernie had a knack for turning a simple hello into an extended dialogue.

Berkley crossed the lot with Sasha following behind. Halfway up the switchback stairs that led to the second floor apartments, he paused, looking back at his friend. "The bathroom. Has it been … ?"

"The landlord took care of everything," Sasha said. "Cleaned up, fresh paint. I made sure of it."

Of course she did. Sasha had been taking care of Berkley since they first met at Spartanburg High School sophomore year. A natural nurturer, she had come to his defense when some of the jocks were picking on him, and she hadn't stopped looking out for him over the past sixteen years. At times it could be a bit overbearing, but he'd be lying if he didn't admit it was also comforting. A human security blanket.

Steeling himself with a few deep breaths, he continued up the stairs until he stood on the landing at the door to his apartment. 2B, the tarnished brass B slightly crooked as it had been since he first moved in. Just as it dawned on Berkley that he didn't have his keys on him, Sasha held out the spare he'd given her years ago.

"Thanks," he said, taking the key and slipping it into the lock. He hesitated a few more seconds, long enough to silently chastise himself for such melodramatic behavior, then unlocked the door.

He took only a few steps inside, barely enough for Sasha to slip in behind him and close the door. The overcast day allowed little light to filter in through the apartment's lone window so that the one-room studio seemed draped with a blanket of shadow. At least until Sasha flipped the light switch, the overhead bulb chasing away the shadows with its glaring brightness.

Berkley took a moment to simply gaze around the room as if he'd never seen the place before. In truth, that was sort of how he felt. The apartment that had once been comfortable and familiar now seemed strange and alien. The tiny kitchen area to his right, separated from the rest of the space by a short bar; the Murphy bed that could fold into the wall but which he always kept down; the far corner with the thrift store sofa and chair and his old Cathode Ray Tube television (Sasha called it a "big butt TV"); the heating/air unit underneath the window, looking like the kind of unit you would find in transitory motels. Less than five hundred square feet, and it contained his whole world. A week ago the place had felt like a sanctuary and haven, his own little nest, but now looking at it as with new eyes, it seemed almost pathetic. Fine for the twenty-five year old he'd been when he first moved in, but for a thirty-two year old to still be living in this kind of bohemian squalor reeked of arrested development.

"Home sweet home, huh?" Sasha said from behind him.

"Something like that," he said, walking further into the room. He sat on the bed; the mattress was as lumpy as ever, but he had to admit it felt better than that hospital bed.

Sasha stepped around the bar into the kitchen. "Hungry? I could fix you something to eat?"

"I don't think there's much here to fix. Old Mother Hubbard's got nothing on me."

Sasha opened the refrigerator to reveal a display of items. "I might have stocked you up on supplies this morning."

Berkley did another quick scan of the apartment, this time noting the made bed, the lack of dust build-up, the neatly stacked magazines on the coffee table. No clothes strewn on the floor by the bed, no dirty dishes in the sink.

"I take it you straightened up a bit as well?" he asked.

Another one-shoulder shrug. "Thought it might be nice to come home to a clean apartment."

Berkley nodded, thinking perhaps that was one of the reasons the place felt so unfamiliar. He hadn't seen it this spotless in a long while. Turning to the bedside table, which had been dusted and perhaps even polished, he noticed something missing. The little music box that Kevin had given him. Of course Sasha would have scoured the apartment to remove all reminders of Kevin. She knew him better than anyone, and she would have wanted to spare him any unpleasant associations.

Glancing at the closed bathroom door, he realized that such a task was impossible as unpleasant associations would be unavoidable anytime he needed to take a piss. Which he did right now, but he held it. Postponing the inevitable.

"How about I make a big pot of spaghetti?" Sasha said, already taking the noodles and sauce out of a cabinet above the stove. "I'm not exactly Gordon Ramsey, but I think even with my limited culinary skills I can't screw up spaghetti."

"Shouldn't you be getting home?"

Sasha squatted down out of sight and rummaged around in a lower cabinet, finally popping back up with a large dented pot. "I figure if you don't want to have a slumber party at my place, we'll have one here."

"You really don't have to do that."

"I know I don't *have* to, but I *want* to. You shouldn't be alone your first night back."

Berkley opened his mouth to argue some more, but

then he closed it again without saying a word. It might be nice to have some company. He didn't really want to talk about what had happened with Kevin, but he knew Sasha would be sensitive enough not to force him, instead waiting until he was ready to discuss it.

Which would be never.

"I like my spaghetti extra saucy," Berkley said, pushing up off the bed.

Sasha raised a hand to her forehead in a comical salute. "Chef Sasha is on the case."

As she placed the pot in the sink and began to fill it with water, Berkley shuffled toward the bathroom. He felt Sasha's eyes on his back, and his hand shook as he reached for the knob. He wondered if it would be insane to hustle over to the convenience store down the street to use their restroom.

Of course it would, and he was in danger of peeing in his pants if he didn't go soon.

Pushing into the bathroom and kicking the door closed behind him, his eyes surveyed the room quickly. The fresh paint was obvious but hid whatever stains there might have been. The shower curtain was pulled closed, hiding his view of the tub.

Unzipping, he closed his eyes and relieved his aching bladder. He tried not to think of what had happened in this room.

And found himself thinking of nothing else.

2: Bubble Bath

Berkley lowered himself into the tub, submerging his body in the luxuriously warm water and mountains of sudsy bubbles, careful to hold the book out of the way of any splashing that might dampen the pages. Sasha often made fun of his proclivity for bubble baths, had even taken to calling him Calgon on occasion, and she definitely didn't understand reading in the tub where a single slip of the fingers could ruin the book. Yet Berkley found reading in the bath extremely relaxing.

And he was in desperate need of relaxation at the moment.

He cracked open the book, The Deep *by Nick Cutter, and began reading the first chapter. He'd picked up this title at the bookstore last night based on his supervisor Zane's recommendation, and Berkley hoped it would be as engrossing as promised. Zane's recs could go either way. They'd suggested Joe Hill's* NOS4A2 *which Berkley had loved, but they had also recommended* House of Leaves, *a book Berkley thought could aptly be described as a migraine captured on paper.*

After only the first few pages, Berkley decided this one might be a winner because he found himself having that unique experience reading gave to him when the story was good. Sort of an astral projection where he forgot his own body and dove mind-first into the world of the fiction. Books had always provided an escape from reality for him, which was why he had always wanted to work at a bookstore. Of course, that experience turned out not to be exactly as he had imagined it and sometimes was the very reality he used books to escape, but it paid the bills. Barely.

Berkley had made it to chapter five, not even noticing the water had cooled from warm to lukewarm and was on its way to cold, when the buzzing of his cell phone pulled his attention out of the story. He glanced over at the toilet, where the phone rested on the closed lid, and wondered why he hadn't turned the damn thing off instead of merely setting it to vibrate. Could be Sasha calling, though she normally texted, or Zane wanting to see if Berkley could cover someone else's shift. Might be Ernie, feeling the itch to chat, or even possibly a wrong number.

But no, Berkley knew even without looking at the screen that it was Kevin. Of course it was Kevin.

Since Berkley had broken up with Kevin via text message last week, the man had called and texted no less than a hundred times. His messages were rambling and vacillated between morose and angry. Some were filled with promises, others with threats. All of them were scary.

Berkley didn't know how he could have gotten involved with someone so mentally unstable.

Only that was a lie; he did know. It was that dimpled smile, the crystalline blue eyes, and those tight jeans. In fact, it was the jeans that had first gotten Berkley's attention, or at least the merchandise those jeans had so perfectly displayed. Berkley had been shelving books at the store when he'd turned a corner and got his first glimpse of that ass, perfectly filling out the seat of those jeans. Berkley asked the man if he could help him find something, and Kevin had turned, flashing those eyes and that smile.

And Berkley had been hooked, a full-blown addict with Kevin as his drug. What followed was a three-month affair both passionate and tumultuous. Kevin had a volatile temper and could become irrationally jealous over even the smallest things, including some that existed only in his fevered imagination.

The inevitable culmination occurred when Kevin became convinced that while the two were driving through downtown Spartanburg on the way to the NGC movie theater Berkley had winked at some young bleached-blonde walking down the street. Berkley called Kevin crazy, which only further escalated the situation, and at a red light Kevin lashed out and punched Berkley in the side of the face. There had been pain, but mostly shock and disbelief. And fear.

Kevin immediately began crying and apologizing, and Berkley had gone along with it, assuring forgiveness, but only to keep Kevin calm. Berkley got out of the movie by claiming his head hurt too much, and Kevin drove him back to his apartment. Kevin hadn't wanted to leave, insisting he should spend the night. Berkley finally convinced the man that he needed sleep and they could try the movie again the next night.

As soon as Kevin was gone, Berkley called Sasha who came straight over and was with him as he texted Kevin, telling him it was over.

Except it wasn't over for Kevin, who started his barrage of calls and texts. He'd even shown up at the store earlier this evening, causing a bit of a scene before finally storming out. Luckily Zane proved understanding, having gone through their own abusive relationship in the past.

Sasha thought Berkley should report the assault and get a restraining order, but Berkley just wanted it all to go away. And figured given enough time Kevin would lose interest and find someone else over which to obsess.

When the phone finally stopped buzzing, Berkley tried to return to The Deep *but found his ability to concentrate on the words had fled. Closing the book, he placed it on the rim of the tub and closed his eyes. Maybe a nap would do him good. Sasha would be horrified to know he sometimes fell asleep in the bath, but there was no danger of him drowning. The tub was so small, he really had to wedge himself into the tight space with his legs severely bent. He had grown used to the positioning so the discomfort didn't prevent him from napping, but now he became aware of the rapidly cooling water and knew he'd never be able to drift off this way.*

His eyes snapped open when he thought he heard the click of his front door opening, but he quickly dismissed the idea, realizing it must be Ernie next door either coming or going. These apartments were so small and the walls so thin, sound carried from one to the other as if everything were happening in your own space.

Berkley reached for the book again, figuring he'd give it one more go, but his hand froze when a soft tinkling music filled the air, a tinny version of "I Will Always Love You." The song the music box Kevin had given him on their second date played. The music box still sitting on the table next to his bed.

Berkley gripped the edges of the tub, beginning to pull himself up, when Kevin suddenly filled the bathroom door, hair sticking up in wild greasy tufts and corkscrews, pale eyes wide and unfocused. Berkley let out a squeak and dropped back into the tub, upending the Cutter book which splashed through the bubbles and water. "What the fuck are you doing here?" Berkley said, sickened by how weak and whiny the question came out.

Kevin did not answer at first, his chest heaving with deep breaths, his jaw set so tight Berkley wouldn't have been surprised if he pulverized his teeth from the tension. Finally he said, his voice much more firm than Berkley's, "We need to talk."

"No, you need to get out of here before I call the –
"

Berkley had been preparing to rise again but everything stopped – movement, speech, thought – when Kevin raised his right hand and Berkley got a look at the gun.

"Please, just hear me out," Kevin said, his voice surprisingly casual as he stepped fully into the cramped bathroom and closed the door behind him, as if needing privacy from the rest of the empty apartment. "I've got a lot to say."

Berkley settled back into the tub. He felt the saturated book bump against his hip but he made no move to retrieve it. The thing was ruined, and he had more important matters to worry about right now. He glanced over at the toilet, at his cell phone, but as if reading his mind, Kevin picked up the cell, lifted the toilet lid, and let the phone drop into water. Kevin then calmly lowered the lid again and took a seat on top of it. The gun hand rested on his thigh, the gun itself still pointed directly at Berkley. Kevin's finger remained curled around the trigger.

"How did you get in here?" Berkley asked, gathering the mounds of bubbles around himself as if they could somehow shield him if bullets started to fly.

A smile curled Kevin's plump lips, as if they were simply reminiscing about good times. "Remember last month when you lent me your key so I could let myself in to make you dinner while you were at work? Well, I might have stopped by Ace Hardware and had a copy made."

Last month? Well before they had broken up. Why had he been making secret duplicate keys then? Had he been anticipating the breakup and this very moment?

"I've spent almost every night this past week

standing outside your apartment. Hell, one night I let myself in and watched you sleep for a while."

Berkley's blood turned colder than the bath water at the idea that Kevin had been in his apartment while he slept, standing over him, maybe even holding the gun. He considered screaming for help, all the neighbors were sure to hear, but Kevin could pull the trigger faster than any of them could react.

"I'm sorry that I hurt you, I never meant to," Berkley said, trying to pass off the tremor in his voice as the emotion of regret rather than fear. "I got scared. I'd never gotten as close to anyone as I did you, and it freaked me out a little. No one tells you how terrifying love can be."

Kevin laughed, but there was no mirth in the sound. It came out dry, like a cough. "You don't love me. If you did, you never could have thrown me over because of one little impulsive action on my part."

Berkley remembered the shock of the punch, the belated realization that he'd hitched his wagon to a dangerous man, but he said nothing, his mind whirring as he tried to think of a way out of this situation.

Kevin leaned forward suddenly, causing Berkley to cringe against the back of the tub. As Kevin spoke, he gestured with the gun, waving it around though the barrel remained pointed in Berkley's direction. Berkley felt his bladder let loose.

"Don't you see, I hit you because I love you," Kevin said. "Because I knew you didn't love me back. I saw the way you were always flirting with other guys, even girls sometimes. Doing it right in front of me, like you were flaunting how little I meant to you. How much do you expect a man to take of that sort of thing before he has to

react? I think you were trying to give me a reason to hit you so that you could justify breaking things off."

Berkley could have denied all that, but he knew it would do no good. Kevin was deluded, and he would not be convinced that his beliefs held no actual relationship to reality.

"What finally made me decide I needed to come in here and talk to you," he continued, *"was what happened at the store tonight. Not you telling me to get out and that you never wanted to see me again, but what happened after I left. I hung around outside for a minute, and I looked through the window and saw you hugging Zane. I realized then that you had a thing for him."*

"Them," Berkley corrected automatically.

Kevin rolled his eyes. *"Oh yeah, non-binary. He or she or it or what-the-hell-ever, I could see that you had moved on."*

"Zane is a friend, that's all. They were only trying to make me feel better after –"

"Stop lying to me!" Kevin shouted, jumping to his feet and holding the gun straight out. *"After everything, the very least you owe me is the truth."*

"Okay, okay, okay," Berkley said, deciding to change tactics. Reason would obviously be of no help, so maybe if he played into Kevin's delusions he might find an escape route. *"Yes, I fell in love with Zane. I didn't mean to, and I foolishly thought breaking up with you the way I did would be an easier let down than admitting I had someone else in my life."*

A sigh shuddered through Kevin and he settled back on the toilet, though the gun's aim never wavered. *"At least you're finally coming clean. That's something."*

"You deserve better than me, Kev."

A sob burst from Kevin's throat like a mini-explosion. "You're the only one for me. I knew that the second we met in the bookstore. It was instant, not like we were meeting for the first time but reuniting. I had never really believed in the concept of soulmates until that moment."

Berkley began shivering so severely that it caused his teeth to chatter, but it wasn't just the cold water causing this full-body chill. How could he have dated this man for three months and somehow missed this insanity? Berkley hated to admit it, but he'd been blinded by the sex. Almost addicted to it. And like most addictions, it had proven dangerous. Potentially lethal.

"Everything's screwed up now," Kevin said. "It can't be salvaged, I know that. But I also know that I can't spend the rest of my life without my soulmate. Would be like trying to live without a heart. I guess the most I can hope for is that we can get it right in the next life."

"I don't believe in reincarnation," Berkley said without thinking.

Kevin laughed again. "You don't believe in reincarnation. I didn't believe in soulmates. Guess this relationship has been a real education for both of us. Maybe we'll be able to implement what we've learned the next time around."

Kevin's tone became more and more mournful, and Berkley did not think that could bode well. All calculation and planning fled his mind, and he was left with nothing but desperate pleading. "Kev, please put down the gun."

Kevin glanced at the gun in his hand quizzically, as if only now realizing he held it. "Oh, the gun isn't for you. I mean, I needed to make sure you would hear me out so you'd understand why I'm doing what I'm doing, but the gun is for me."

"What? No, Kev, you don't want to hurt yourself."

"I don't want any of this, but it's what I have to do."

"You don't have to. Listen to me, you don't have to do any of this. Despite everything, I still care about you. I don't want you to hurt yourself, and you surely wouldn't want me to have to watch you do something like that."

Another quizzical frowned tugged at the corners of Kevin's mouth. "You won't have to watch."

Kevin lunged forward abruptly, giving Berkley no time to react. Kevin placed his hands on Berkley's shoulders and pushed, shoving Berkley under the water. Berkley flailed and beat against the side of the tub, trying to thrust himself back up, but his hands and feet slipped and slid. He began to beat at Kevin's hands, but he may as well have been beating at the stone hands of a statue.

For a second, Kevin's grip did seem to lessen and Berkley's nose broke the surface. He tried to take a quick inhale but mostly got a snoot full of strawberry-scented bubbles before being plunged back beneath the water. He felt the book against his side and grabbed it, hoping to use it as a weapon, but when he lifted it, the waterlogged volume slapped against the side of Kevin's head then fell ineffectually from his fingers.

Berkley continued to struggle, his survival instincts kicking in, and he took hold of Kevin's hands that held him under water, trying to dig his nails into the flesh. He could feel the sharp metal of the gun still in Kevin's hand and tried to pry it lose, but the angle was awkward and he found him strength waning as his lungs cried out for oxygen.

He flashed back to his earlier thought that it was

impossible to drown in this tub and redoubled his efforts to get his head above water.

Yet his efforts went unrewarded. Through the wavering water and dissipating bubbles, he could see the distorted image of Kevin's face. It was not twisted with malice or fury. His face actually appeared tranquil, which was somehow even more terrifying.

Berkley held out as long as he could, but finally he opened his mouth and convulsively breathed in a great gulp of the bath water.

3: The Fallen Books

Berkley awoke with a start. The nightmare clung to him like the phantom strands of a spider web. He imagined he could still taste the bubbles in his mouth and feel his body submerged in the water. He was soaked, that much wasn't a dream, night sweats having saturated his pajamas and sheets. He must not have cried out in his sleep, however, because Sasha still slumbered next to him, snoring softly.

Moving gingerly as not to disturb her, he slipped out of bed and padded across the dark apartment to the kitchen area. He took the slightly crusty hand towel that hung on the oven door handle and wiped the perspiration from his face then filled a glass of water at the sink.

He stared across the room at the bathroom door. Sasha had taken a rinse in the shower right before they turned in and she'd left the door open, so that now it yawned wide like the mouth of a beast that wanted to swallow him whole. Berkley took only a sip of the water then poured the rest down the drain, trying to shake off the remnants of the nightmare.

Nightmare? More like memories, playing through my subconscious mind like mental home movies of some traumatic event. What does it say about my life when my memories are nightmare material?

Berkley glanced at the clock on the stove, which Sasha must have actually set while he was in the hospital since it used to only flash zeroes. Half past three a.m. Despite being bone-weary, he knew he wasn't likely to get back to sleep tonight. Couldn't exactly watch TV as it would wake Sasha. He went to the tall six-shelf bookcase against the wall beside the door to his small balcony, stopping along the way to switch on the floor lamp next to the living room chair. At the bookcase, he scanned the titles. No sign of *The Deep*. His copy had been ruined of course and no doubt thrown out by Sasha or the landlord. Berkley knew he would never attempt to read it again, or anything by Nick Cutter for that matter, now having unfortunate associations with the book and author.

After perusing spines for another minute, he plucked a book from the bottom shelf. *Disappearing Act* by Bradley Storm. Berkley had never read this author before, and in fact this book was an advanced reader's copy he'd snagged from the store over a year ago because it had sounded vaguely interesting. He had never gotten around to reading it, but hopefully it would help him while away the remaining hours of darkness.

With his feet tucked underneath him, Berkley settled in the chair, leaning into the meager light provided by the lamp. He opened the book to the first chapter and began reading. Or tried to. His eyes scanned the first line, moved on to the second, realized he hadn't really registered the first, went back and scanned it again, still failed to ascertain the meaning of the words arranged in that particular order. He recognized this was no fault of the author's, but his mind couldn't focus on the page. Instead, it kept returning to the nightmare, to the memory, to the horror that had invaded his life.

The horror hadn't stopped with his drowning. Of course, he had learned the rest later, after he woke up in the hospital. After holding Berkley under water for several minutes, Kevin had put the gun in his mouth and pulled the trigger, splattering the contents of his head all over the bathroom wall. The gunshot had brought Ernie hurrying over from next door, where he'd found the apartment door standing open. After calling 911, Ernie had pulled Berkley out of the tub and performed CPR (chest compressions and mouth-to-mouth) until he jumpstarted Berkley's heart. Ernie had then rolled Berkley over onto his side where he'd coughed up copious amounts of the water that had filled his lungs.

Just shy of five minutes. That was how long they think Berkley was clinically dead. Five minutes with no heartbeat, no breath, until Ernie had restored both. Imagine if his neighbor hadn't been home that night?

I guess I was murdered, if you want to get technical about it. Kevin didn't merely attempt murder; he actually succeeded. Unfortunately for him it didn't take, unlike his suicide. Even all the King's horses and all the King's men couldn't put the eggshell of his skull back together again.

Berkley tried again to lose himself in the novel, a historical story theorizing a supernatural explanation for the lost colony of Roanoke. Normally he didn't read a lot of historical fiction, but perhaps that was exactly what he needed right now. Leave behind everything familiar about the modern world and delve into a past that had no connection to his current life.

Or so he thought. At the beginning of chapter two, a young girl drowned in the Croatan Sound. The author described the drowning in excruciating detail, and that hit a little too close to home for Berkley. He closed the book with a snap then heard a soft clattering from behind him. A glance over his shoulder didn't immediately reveal the source of the noise. Only when he stood up did he spot the books on the floor.

Stepping to the bookcase, Berkley knelt and slid the copy of *Disappearing Act* back into its slot on the shelf then gathered up the three paperbacks that had fallen. *The Bell Jar* by Sylvia Plath, *Mrs. Dalloway* by Virginia Woolf, and *The Old Man and the Sea* by Ernest Hemmingway. Berkley stood, staring down at the books with confusion.

He could understand if removing the Storm novel had disrupted the other titles on that shelf, causing a few to fall, but these three were not from the same shelf as *Disappearing Act*. In fact, they all came from the very top shelf, what he thought of as his "Pretension Display." This shelf housed all the classic novels that would look impressive to visitors (a lot of Dickens and Austen, Steinbeck and Fitzgerald) but which he'd never actually read. And likely never would. They existed simply to make him look smarter than he actually was.

As he reached up to replace the books, he noted that they hadn't even been sitting side by side, and since they were paperbacks, they sat far back from the edge of the shelf. He couldn't figure out what could have caused them to fall.

"What're you doing?"

The soft voice caused him to jump and let out a surprised squeal. He'd almost forgotten that Sasha was here, and he turned to see her sitting up in bed, her hair a tangled mess.

"Nothing," Berkley answered in a whisper. "Go back to sleep."

"Needa pee," she mumbled, scooting across the mattress and disappearing into the bathroom.

Berkley returned to the chair. If he couldn't read, he'd sit, stare at the wall, and wait for morning. Maybe he could take up meditation. It was supposed to empty your mind or something. Of course he already felt fairly empty. Perhaps he needed to find something to fill him up again.

The toilet flushed, and Sasha emerged from the bathroom, yawning expressively. Spotting Berkley, she came over and plopped down on the end of the sofa closest to him.

"Don't let my insomnia keep you up," he said.

"I promised you a slumber party. We haven't even braided each other's hair yet."

Berkley ran a hand through his short locks. "Don't think I have enough to braid."

"Maybe not, but we could do cornrows. At the very least, I could put in some extensions."

"Sweetie, I love you, but maybe you can start by just running a brush through your own hair."

Sasha laughed. "Yeah, I caught a glimpse of myself in the mirror and had to stifle a scream. Looks like I put my fingers in an electrical socket or something."

Berkley tilted his head and studied her for a moment. "To me it looks more like you have a giant starfish on your head."

"I went to bed with my hair wet, which is always a big mistake. I'll have to wash it again in the morning just to get it to lie down flat so I can do something with it."

"It is morning."

She glanced over toward the kitchen where the stove clock glowed neon-green. "Jesus, I have to be at work in less than four hours. I'm going to be dead on my feet."

"Call out."

"I've been out the last few days. Need to go back sometime."

Berkley nodded, reminding himself that unlike himself and Jeffrey, Sasha had a real grown-up kind of job. She worked Accounts Payable for a manufacturing plant in the neighboring town of Inman. Sometimes it was hard to reconcile the wild child he knew in their teen years with the responsible young woman across from him now. Of course, at her core she hadn't changed, but she'd matured with age whereas Berkley hadn't. He found himself wondering if she'd end up marrying Jeffrey, having kids. He couldn't imagine their friendship would survive her settling down into that kind of domesticity. She'd become entrenched in family life and leave him all alone.

Would that really be all that different? She's sitting right next to me this second, and I still feel utterly alone.

"Since we're both up anyway, how about I rustle us up some pancakes?" Sasha said. "I can make them into animal shapes."

"You always say that, but the only animal you seem to be able to make is an amoeba."

Sasha reached across the space between them to swat his arm then got up to head into the kitchen. Berkley laughed, but he didn't feel particularly jovial. He went through the motions of their usual banter, but it was rote, by the numbers. Like he was playing at being himself.

But if I'm not myself then who am I? Am I anybody?

Berkley thought about the card he'd brought home from the hospital, the one now in the junk drawer next to the kitchen sink. Dr. Mirza had given it to him, the card for a psychologist who specialized in Post-Traumatic Stress cases. The physician thought Berkley could benefit from talking to someone. At the time, he'd taken the card as a courtesy, never expecting he'd actually consider going to see a counselor.

But sitting in his apartment which felt like a coffin, watching his best friend who felt like a stranger make a meal he didn't have an appetite for, feeling like an imposter in his own life ... well, he still wasn't ready to make the call but he was at least ready to consider it.

4: The Shredded Pages

At a quarter to noon, Berkley stood outside Page to Page, Spartanburg's lone independent bookstore located right downtown on Main Street. People walked past him, alone or in pairs or in groups, talking or texting or playing games on their phones (was Pokemon Go still a thing?), none of them paying him the slightest attention. A few browsers had stopped to peruse the library cart full of dollar books placed on the sidewalk, others at the handful of outdoor tables, sipping their drinks as cars zipped by and a breeze stirred the day's heat like a soup.

Berkley waited another five minutes, pretending to study the YA display in the front window, stalling so he didn't have to go inside.

Of course, he didn't even have to be here. Zane had told him to take all the time he needed before returning to work. Tempting, but the truth was that if he didn't work, he didn't get paid. If he didn't get paid, he couldn't afford to cover his rent or bills or diet of frozen pizzas and Ramen. He lived cheaply, but his lifestyle still required at least a minimal cash flow.

As it was, this first week back Zane had only scheduled Berkley for half shifts which was going to require some financial juggling.

When he could put off the inevitable no longer, Berkley pushed through the door. The air-conditioned interior was downright chilly, instantly raising goosebumps on his arms. The bookstore consisted of a large open space, the checkout counter immediately to the left, most of the walls lined with bookshelves and more gondola units running in parallel rows down the center. Page to Page sold both new and used books, the new being housed up front and the used in the back. A doorway in the back right corner led to the employee break room and manager's office, and a hallway next to the checkout counter to the small café that sold a variety of coffee drinks, pastries, and even a few sandwiches. Maybe not much compared to the large Barnes & Noble near the interstate, but for the past decade Berkley had called this place his home-away-from-home.

He spotted Annette behind the counter, checking out a customer with an armful of used titles. The new books looked nice, but the secondhand selection was what really moved and kept the lights on. That and the coffee. In the breakroom, some jokester had put up a sign that read, "Thank God for Addictive Legal Beverages!"

Avoiding eye contact with Annette, Berkley made his way through the store toward the breakroom. He recognized a few of the store's regulars, prowling the aisles in search of that perfect book. He received a nod or two in acknowledgment, but no one showed any particular concern. Perhaps they had no idea what had happened to him, why he'd been out of work. Of course, Zane would be sensitive enough not to want that kind of personal information to get out. It was possible that even Annette and the other booksellers didn't know, though less likely.

In the breakroom, Berkley went to the time clock, the old-fashioned kind where you literally punched a card. Just the kind of nostalgia Page to Page traded in. He found his card, punched the clock, and turned to find Zane standing in the doorway to their office. The two merely stared at one another for a moment, playing a strange game of chicken that would never end since neither of them were moving.

"So," Zane said at last, "you sure you're ready for this?"

"If I wasn't here, I'd just be at home with way too much time for thinking."

Zane grimaced. "Thinking, yikes! You're right, no one needs an excess of time for that."

"Thanks for the flowers you had sent to the hospital, by the way."

"No problem. I should have come visit, I know, but hospitals give me the creeps."

"I don't blame you. I wouldn't have been there if I hadn't had to be."

Zane shifted from one foot to the other, clearly uncomfortable. Berkley wished they would go back in their office and close the door, put an end to both their suffering, but Zane seemed to think small talk was necessary to normalize the situation. "I like your shirt," they said.

Berkley glanced down at his chest, as if he didn't know what he was wearing. As if he hadn't spent several minutes this morning staring into his closet, wondering why a thirty-five year old man's wardrobe consisted of almost nothing but graphic Ts. He'd chosen this one, depicting the character of Death from the comic series *Sandman*, featuring her trademark ankh and the quote, "You get what everyone gets ... you get a lifetime."

"Thanks," Berkley said. "We have any sales going on?"

"Yeah, we do actually. The Spartanburg Country schoolboard is considering banning *To Kill a Mockingbird* because of pressure from some concerned parents group, so we have it and *Go Tell a Watchman* thirty percent off."

One corner of Berkley's mouth lifted in a half-smile. "Nice. Should I take over for Annette at the register?"

"No, we had a bunch of used books donated

yesterday. If you could get those shelved, that would be great. If you don't finish today, no big deal."

Berkley nodded, itching to get out from under Zane's obvious concern and sympathy. He found it grating. He started from the room but then Zane came over tand gave him a hug. Berkley didn't exactly return the embrace, but he endured it. It would have been rude to do otherwise.

Finally Zane pulled away. "I'm so sorry this happened to you."

"Not your fault," Berkley said, thinking that it had in fact been another hug between he and Zane that had been the catalyst for Kevin's deadly actions. Of course, that was merely pretense; if it hadn't been Zane, it would have been something else. "Everyone warned me there was something off about Kevin. You, Sasha, even my neighbor Ernie. I didn't listen, and that's on me."

"Well, if you need anything, don't hesitate to ask."

"I appreciate that," Berkley said. "Only thing I need is to keep busy. When you make out the schedule for next week, would you mind putting me back to my regular hours?"

"If you're sure."

"I am. I don't want to lose my full-time senior bookseller status."

"Then you got it," Zane said and gave him another brief hug. "It's great to have you back."

Berkley wasn't sure whether or not Zane was aware of the possible double meaning of their well-wishes, but he replied, "It's great to be back."

Not at all sure if he meant it.

*

Berkley wheeled his cart over to the used nonfiction, which took up half of the back wall. As he

2B

began shelving, readjusting the books to make rooms for the new arrivals, he lost himself in the task. He knew some considered this kind of work boring, but Berkley found the repetitive monotony somehow relaxing, almost therapeutic. He could get caught up in the rhythm to the point that all other thought completely left his mind. He wasn't even really a person, more an automaton, a robot who existed only to perform a specific function. He understood why that sort of depersonalization would not appeal to others, but especially right now he needed it.

"Excuse me, do you work here?"

Berkley reluctantly looked over at the customer, a high-school aged girl, and forced a smile. It felt so unnatural on his face that he could practically hear the creaking of his lips. "Yes. Can I help you with something?"

"Yeah, my mother's birthday is coming up and I want to get her something by this writer she likes. Joyce Carol Oates."

"We have a wide selection in Literary Fiction," Berkley said, turning back to his cart.

"I looked and couldn't find any."

Berkley closed his eyes and forced himself not to sigh audibly. He didn't appreciate this girl interrupting his flow, reminding him that he was a person and not a robot, but she was a customer and therefore he couldn't exactly tell her to buzz off. He kept repeating to himself the retail mantra: *customer's always right, customer's always right, customer's always right*. The mantra was bullshit, of course, but bullshit was the cornerstone of retail.

"Let me see if I can locate them for you," he said and started toward the front of the store, not bothering to make sure the girl followed.

He zeroed in on the books immediately. A shelf and

35

a half of Joyce Carol Oates books, some of them with the covers facing out. He wanted to tell the girl they were impossible to miss, but instead he held out his hand and said, "Here you are."

"How embarrassing," the girl said with a laugh. "I was looking under C for Carol instead of O for Oates. Guess I thought it was a hyphenated name or something."

"Happens," Berkley said and started walking away.

"Do you know which of these is the most recent release?"

This time Berkley wasn't able to completely suppress the sigh. "I don't. Maybe check the copyright pages."

Before the girl could ask any more inane questions, he hurried back through the store. As he came around the last gondola, he nearly collided with Zane's back.

"Sup, boss?" Berkley said, afraid Zane had heard how dismissive he'd been with the customer.

But Zane's attention seemed focused elsewhere. "What happened?" they asked.

"I was helping someone find – "

"No, I mean what happened *here*?"

Berkley followed Zane's gaze to his cart, the books still stacked up on the top. Except for one. One book was now on the floor, shredded.

And shredded was definitely the right word. The pages had not only been ripped out, but then torn into little confetti pieces that littered the floor like a paper snowfall. Like a wild beast had gotten its claws into the book.

"Who did this?" Zane asked.

Berkley looked around the nearby aisles but saw no one. "I don't know. I went to find a book for a customer, but I was gone less than a minute I swear."

Zane looked dubious but also like they thought they couldn't yell at Berkley right now, not after the ordeal he'd been through. "Well, I'd say this book is beyond salvage. Can you clean this mess up?"

"Sure," Berkley said, kneeling down to start scooping up the paper.

"By the way, what book is it?"

Berkley picked up the remnants of the book's cover and felt an inexplicable chill trickle down his spine like a drop of cold water. "*Dr. Death.* That book about Jack Kevorkian."

5: Suicidal CDs

Berkley pulled up in front of his apartment building at half past four that afternoon, amazed that he could feel this drained after only four hours of work. His exhaustion was not physical, but mental. Spiritual, even. All that interaction with customers, asking questions, wanting help, suffocating him with their neediness. Zane's obtrusive nurturing only added to the strain. Annette had repeatedly tried to engage him in conversation. She had one of those high-pitched squeaky voices where the inflection went up at the end of every sentence, making statements sound like questions, and it jabbed into Berkley's brain like an icepick behind the eyes.

He'd thought returning to work would be a restoration of normalcy, or at least a nice distraction. Instead, it had succeeded only in making him feel even more out of step with normal life. After a day like this, he once would have wanted nothing more than to soak in a bubble bath, but of course he doubted he'd ever take a bath again. And showering didn't have quite the same de-stressing effect. He'd have to settle for his bed, a bag of Doritos, and something mindless playing on the TV. After all that forced social interaction at the store, he looked forward to simply being alone.

Halfway up the stairs that scaled the front of the building like an exoskeleton, he heard a door open and glanced up to see his neighbor stepping out of 2A. Ernie's face, which Berkley sometimes thought of as a boxer's face with its square shape and bent nose and overhanging brow, usually looked severe or even angry (resting bitch face wasn't exclusive to women), but now it was relaxed into something almost beatific. Berkley couldn't quite identify the expression. Seemed a mixture of anxiety, caring, and something akin to relief.

"Hey there, Berk," the man said.

"Hi, Ernie. You heading out?"

"What? Oh no, I heard your car pull up and thought I'd say hello, see how you were doing."

At the top of the stairs, Berkley mimicked Sasha's signature half-shrug. "Getting by as best I can. Everything's a little weird right now."

"I can only imagine. I thought about popping over last night but figured you might need the night to settle back in."

"I appreciate that," Berkley said then realized he owed him appreciation for more than giving him space his first night back from the hospital. "And thank you for…well, you know. Jesus, I don't know how you properly thank someone for saving your life. A 'Thank You' card hardly seems adequate. I'd offer you my car, but that thing is cheaper than a card."

Ernie flapped a dismissive hand. "You don't owe me anything. Anyone would have done the same. I'm just glad I took that CPR course at the YMCA."

"Me too," Berkley said, inserting his key into the door's lock.

Ernie stepped closer. "Mind if I come in for a minute?"

Berkley turned the key until he heard the *cluck* of the lock disengaging then paused. He wanted to say no, that he wasn't up for company, but not only would that be rude – it would be almost abnormal. A normal human being would not hesitate to invite the person who saved his or her life in, offer them coffee, that sort of thing. Perhaps the key to Berkley shaking off this apathy and feeling like a normal human being again was to start acting like one.

"Be my guest," Berkley said, opening the door and letting Ernie go in first.

When Berkley followed him in, Ernie turned to him and said, "I think you left the water running somewhere."

Berkley heard it as well, the trickling sound of a faucet letting out a steady stream. He followed the sound into the bathroom and found water dribbling in the tub. Not from the showerhead but from the tub's spigot. He gripped the handle and tightened it, ceasing the flow. Curious, he had taken a shower before leaving for work but had been sure he'd completely turned the water off.

As he stepped away from the tub, his left foot slid in a small puddle of water that had gathered on the tile. He usually toweled off completely before stepping out of the shower, but apparently he'd tracked some water out this morning and not realized it. He grabbed the hand towel on the bar above the toilet and dropped it over the puddle, sopping it up.

He left the bathroom and found Ernie standing in the very center of the apartment, looking around as if the space wasn't an exact replica of his own with different furniture. "Didn't spring a leak, did you?" Ernie asked.

"No, just didn't turn the water completely off I guess. Would you like something to drink?"

"A beer would hit the spot."

"Sure, Sasha stocked me up."

She'd stocked him up with some fancy Belgian beer, Stella Artois. Berkley was more a Bud kind of man, but Sasha constantly tried to elevate his tastes. He took two of the bottles and brought them over to Ernie. The man still scanned the apartment as if looking for something.

The damn bunny! The one I left in the hospital room and which probably got tossed in the trash with the dead flowers from Zane.

Ernie accepted the offered beer with a smile and they took a seat at opposite ends of the sofa. Berkley took a swig of the beer and hated to admit that it tasted amazing, making the Bud he usually drank seem like canned piss. Which was just how Sasha usually referred to it. He would never say as much to her, however.

Silence rolled out between them, filling up the apartment like a noxious gas. Unusual, as Ernie's chatterbox nature usually never left room for even a whiff of silence. Many times he had wished he could make the man shut up, but now that his neighbor seemed uncharacteristically at a loss for words, Berkley found it disconcerting, more evidence that his life was off-kilter like a *Twilight Zone* episode.

"So," Berkley finally said just to banish the silence, "I hear you rode in the ambulance with me to the hospital."

"I didn't think it would be right to let you go alone. I came to visit you later that first day, but you were out of it. Probably didn't know I was there."

"No, I wasn't aware of very much at first. Kind of disoriented and it took me a while to even remember what happened."

"If that bastard hadn't killed himself, I'd have done the job myself," Ernie said, squeezing the bottle so hard Berkley feared the glass might shatter in the man's fist. The vehemence and venom in Ernie's voice surprised Berkley. Despite his neighbor's bulldog appearance, he had always exuded a gentle passivity. This degree of anger was a new layer to the man.

Berkley took another pull from his own bottle, enjoying the smooth flavor as it slid down his throat. "Well, we don't have to worry about Kevin Nix anymore."

"I knew the guy was bad news," Ernie said, sliding over and clamping a hand on Berkley's knee. "But I never thought he'd do something like this. When I think about how close I came to losing you, I just … I mean, I don't know … "

Ernie trailed off, and Berkley looked down at the hand on his knee, wondering if he should take it in his own. No, that might give Ernie the wrong idea, send the wrong message. Berkley had of course known almost since Ernie first moved in next door three years ago that he had the hots for Berkley. He'd never made any overt moves, part of that gentle passivity, but it was clear that he wanted more from Berkley than friendship.

Ernie was nice enough, but Berkley felt no sparks with the man. He was older, probably nearing fifty, his body squat and solid, not fat exactly but pushing it, salt-and-pepper hair not receding but always worn in a severe military-style buzz cut. No, Berkley simply could not imagine anything romantic with this man.

As the seconds ticked by and Ernie didn't remove his hand, it began to feel more and more awkward, like a dead rat on Berkley's knee. He was trying to think of the most tactful way to shake off the hand when noise from the closet caught their attention. A cascading sound of several items falling.

"What was that?" Ernie asked.

Berkley stood, finally dislodging the dead rat from his knee, and went to the closet, opening the accordion door. Nothing seemed disturbed, except three CD cases were on the floor at his feet. Like most of the modern world under the age of sixty, Berkley streamed all his music, but he hadn't been able to bring himself to get rid of the CDs he'd collected in his youth. He didn't really listen to them, but he kept them tucked away on the upper shelf of his closet. Like mementos from his bygone youth. Once he'd found this sentimental and romantic; now it only seemed stupid and pointless, like saving garbage.

Ernie walked to the closet then bent and picked up the CDs. "Hmm, let's see what we have here. Soundgarden, Nirvana, INXS. Someone has a 90s fetish."

"I grew up on the stuff," Berkley said, taking the CDs and placing them back on the top shelf. "My older brother listened to this kind of music so it sort of became the background soundtrack when I was young."

"A 90s fetish and a suicide fetish. I'm learning a lot about you."

Berkley closed the closet door and turned to his neighbor with a frown. "What do you mean, suicide fetish?"

"Those three bands, the lead singers all killed themselves."

Berkley felt dizzy and thought he may have literally swayed on his feet. He flashed on the books that had fallen from his shelf the night before. Plath, Woolf, and Hemmingway. Carbon monoxide, drowning, gunshot to the head. Three writers who died from suicide, and now these three singers. Add in the shredded book at the store, a book about Dr. Jack Kevorkian, also known as the Suicide Doctor. Puzzle pieces came together, though the overall picture remained unclear.

"First the books, now the CDs," he said softly to himself.

"What?" Ernie asked.

"Oh, nothing. Just that I had some books fall off my bookcase last night."

"Sounds like the place might be haunted," Ernie

said with a laugh.

The dizziness intensified and Berkley leaned against the wall to steady himself.

"Oh shit, I don't know what I'm saying," Ernie said, placing a hand on Berkley's arm. "That was a fucked thing to say considering … well, just considering. I'm so sorry."

Berkley took a few deep breaths and straightened up, a strained smile stretching his lips. "It's okay, wasn't you. I'm tired, that's all."

"Seriously though, I do apologize for my big mouth. It was only a joke."

"I know," Berkley said, thinking, *You may have meant it as a joke, but I'm not so sure it is.*

*

Midnight approached, but Berkley didn't sleep. Instead, he sat up in bed, laptop resting across his thighs. All the lights in the apartment were off, only the glow from the screen washing his face in a spectral phosphorescence. Considering the subject he found himself researching online, perhaps he should have turned on a few lights. But no, he doubted the harsh glare from electric bulbs would make any of this less creepy.

The internet provided all the information one could ever want on any topic imaginable. Of course, that didn't mean every piece of information was reliable. That, of course, was the tricky part about the net. You had to weed through all the bullshit to get to the actual kernels of truth.

This weeding process proved even harder when researching the paranormal, where you didn't exactly have much in the way of scientific studies to fall back on. A lot of speculation and conjecture, anecdotes and unreliable eyewitness accounts. There were some videos and photographs, but few that seemed compelling or authentic.

He found one photo of a little British girl supposedly being levitated by a spirit, which many considered some of the best visual evidence of otherworldly occurrences, but to Berkley it was clearly a shot taken of her mid-leap from her bed.

Considering the lack of verifiable facts, he looked for consistencies, things that seemed to remain the same across stories from a variety of people. For instance, a general consensus seemed to be that hauntings happened either when people died in a particularly violent manner, or when people died with unfinished business.

Both theories fit here. Kevin had definitely died in a violent manner, splattering his brains across the bathroom wall. He'd also died with unfinished business in that he'd tried to take Berkley with him and failed.

Regarding communication with a spirit, Berkley found only the usual methods, stuff he'd seen in a million movies. Ouija boards, séances, mediums. In the movies, these attempts to contact the deceased usually ended up making matters worse. However, he had found some testimonials online that suggested sometimes they could be helpful, that merely communicating with a ghost could help it move on.

And if that wasn't enough, how could one get rid of a ghost? He found tales of supposed real-life exorcisms, rituals that involved burning sage and incantations. It all sounded quite goofy, and it made him question what he was even doing, staying up into the wee hours researching ways to talk to and expel ghosts.

Did he really believe that Kevin was haunting him? Seemed absurd, or at least it would when the sun came up and he was around other people again. However, alone in the dark it felt at least possible, if not plausible.

Setting the laptop aside, Berkley stretched and rubbed at his eyes. He had another half shift tomorrow, this one starting at eight a.m., so he should really try to get to sleep. He wasn't overly confident that would happen; he imagined he'd simply lie in bed on high alert for any strange sounds or movements. Still, he had to try. He'd hit the bathroom then attempt to find his way into slumberland.

He stepped into the bathroom, and even as he flipped the light switch, his foot splashed into something wet. He looked down, finding another puddle, this one twice as big as the one from this afternoon. Situated in the very center of the floor making an almost perfect circle, it defied explanation. Berkley hadn't showered again after getting home from work, and he didn't see how it could be the result of a leak since the borders stopped shy of the tub, sink, or toilet.

This puddle was too large for the hand towel, so Berkley squatted down to retrieve one of the larger towels from the cabinet under the sink. He pulled open the doors then paused, for a moment not comprehending the sight that greeted him. Everything in the cabinet – towels, extra rolls of toilet paper, toothpaste tubes, disposable razors – was covered in a slimy pink substance. The slime also coated the sides and top of the inside of the cabinet, dripping down in stringy globs.

Ectoplasm was the first thought that came to Berkley's mind, the viscous residue that he'd read some spirits left in their wake.

But no, as he peered into the back of the cabinet, he realized this substance was not supernatural in nature, though he couldn't account for how it had ended up all over everything under the sink.

It appeared that his bottle of bubble bath had

exploded.

6: Theorizing

Berkley opened the door in the middle of Sasha's second knock. Fist still raised, she looked a little thrown and a lot concerned. "What's going on that I had to stop by on my way to work? Your vaguely cryptic message said it was urgent."

Berkley grabbed her wrist and practically dragged her into the apartment. He knew he must appear manic, a bipolar on the upswing. He kept tugging at his hair, a habit he'd had as a teen when the stress of high school life had left him a mess of nervous tics. He thought he'd outgrown such things … until now.

"You're scaring me," Sasha said. "You look like you've seen a ghost."

This made Berkley laugh, but even that came out a little high-pitched and hysterical. "No, I haven't *seen* one exactly."

"What are you talking about? You're not making any sense."

Berkley had spent the last couple of hours planning what he was going to say to Sasha, how he could broach the subject without sounding like a raving lunatic. He had wanted to ease her into it, but all that went out the window in the moment and he simply blurted, "Kevin is still here."

Sasha's lips quivered as if they didn't know whether to form a smile or a frown, open for a laugh or a scream. "He's still *where*?"

"*Here*, in this apartment. His ghost or spirit or essence or what-the-hell-ever you want to call it. He's haunting this apartment."

Instead of addressing what Berkley had just said, she asked, "Berkley honey, did you sleep at all last night?"

"Actually no, but that's beside the point."

"Or maybe that's exactly the point."

"I know how crazy this sounds," Berkley said. "Believe me, I do. All I ask is that you hear me out, okay?"

Sasha looked skeptical but she nodded.

Berkley led her to the sofa where they sat side by side. He told her about all the strange occurrences since he'd gotten home from the hospital, ending with the most recent one that had happened this morning.

"When I got out of the shower, the mirror was all fogged up from the steam, and there was a clear handprint right in the center."

"Did you happen to take a picture of it?" she asked.

Berkley shook his head. "I still haven't replaced my phone yet. That's why I had to Facebook message you to get you over here. But do you need a picture? Do you think I'm making it up?"

"No," Sasha said, drawing the word out. "However, you could have touched the mirror before you got in the shower this morning or even sometime yesterday and the imprint was still there, waiting to be revealed by the steam."

"What about the bubble bath? How do you explain that?"

Sasha threw up her hands. "I don't know. Maybe it got really hot under the sink or something."

"Have you ever heard of a bottle of bubble bath exploding in the heat?"

"I have not, but I've also never heard about a ghost exploding a bottle of bubble bath either. In fact, I've never heard a credible story about a ghost, period."

"There's a lot of credible stuff online," Berkley said, gesturing toward his laptop which rested on the coffee table in front of them. "It's not all like the silly stuff you see on those ghost hunting shows. Some of what I found is from very reliable sources."

Sasha glanced at the laptop then back at Berkley. "Do you know how some people will go on Web MD and read about some rare and exotic disease then convince themselves they have all the symptoms for it?"

"What the hell does that have to do with anything?"

"All I'm saying is that if you stayed up all night reading about ghostly encounters, isn't it possible that you started taking some random incidents and weaving them into a similar narrative?"

"Random incidents? You make it sound so trivial, like a creaking floorboard or something. That book at the store was torn completely apart."

"Didn't you tell me once that someone took a dump in the bathroom *sink* at the bookstore? You can never underestimate how gross and destructive people are."

"The puddles?"

"Call a plumber."

"What about the books and CDs that fell?" he asked, recognizing the edge of desperation fraying his words. "All of them by artists who killed themselves."

"I admit, that one is a little freaky, but sometimes freaky coincidences do happen in life. I saw a documentary one time about twins separated at birth and adopted by families on opposite ends of the country, and they ended up going to the exact same college and being randomly assigned as roommates their freshman year."

Berkley let loose a growl of frustration. "Sasha, you're not listening to me."

She reached out and took one of his hands, squeezing it between both of hers. "No, I am listening. Now I need you to listen to me. Can you do that?"

Berkley wanted to scream, wanted to tell her to get out, but more than any of that, he wanted her to believe him. He would hear her out then resume trying to convince her. Maybe if he let her speak her peace, she'd be more receptive to his story.

"Fine," he said. "Say what you have to say."

Sasha hesitated for a few seconds, but once she started the words had a rote feel, the whole thing seeming a little rehearsed, as if she'd been practicing this speech for the past twenty-four hours. As if she'd expected … maybe not this exactly but something like this.

"You've been through an ordeal I can't even imagine. That most people could never even imagine. It's not possible that something so traumatic could leave a person unscathed. It would be foolish to think you'd get out of the hospital and then life would just resume as it had been before. I suspect that your life is always going to be broken up into two parts. Life before Kevin did what he did, and life after."

Berkley tried to patiently wait until she was done, but he couldn't help but roll his eyes and say, "You sound like you think you're a therapist instead of an accountant."

"Funny you should bring that up, because it's sort of what I was leading up to. I'm always here if you need to talk, you know that, but maybe you would benefit from talking with a professional."

"So you think I'm crazy?"

"More than psychotics go to therapy," Sasha said. "I mean, I'm in therapy."

This surprised Berkley. He had assumed he knew everything there was to know about Sasha. "How long?"

"Two years now, twice a week."

"Why?" he asked, recognizing too late that the word

held an accusatory note, as if he were really asking, *In what way are you defective?*

"I still have some unresolved issues related to my father."

Berkley knew that her father had been an abusive alcoholic who often took his drunken rages out on Sasha and her mother. However, Sasha usually spoke of her childhood with a snide dark humor that had made him mistakenly assume whatever baggage she carried was empty and light to carry. As it turned out, Kevin hadn't been the only person in his life he didn't fully know.

"I'm sorry," he said. "I didn't realize."

"You don't have to apologize, this isn't about me. I'm telling you so you will see there is no shame in going to see a therapist. We all need a little help and guidance sometimes, and as I said, most of us have never been through anything like what you have."

"I'm dealing," Berkley said, but even he didn't find the words convincing.

"You are, honey, but there's also something missing. The spark that makes you *you*. The quick-witted sarcastic guy that I have been friends with for two decades, I don't see him around here anymore. Dealing seems to be all you're doing, the bare minimum to get by but with nothing else. Again, no spark."

"It has only been a few days. You said yourself, this kind of trauma leaves scars. I can't be expected to just bounce back overnight."

"I know, and I don't expect that," Sasha said. "And I planned to keep this worry to myself, give you time to find your footing, but now you're bringing me this ghost story. And perversely, this is the first time since you woke up in the hospital that I've seen any real vitality in you. The fact that it is over the idea that Kevin is haunting you has me more than a little scared."

Berkley opened his mouth to respond, but when he realized he didn't know what he would say, he closed it again. Sasha made a lot of astute points. He himself had been feeling as if he were sleepwalking through his life, and could it be possible he'd latched on to this haunting idea because it was something different and intriguing enough that it had revived at least an ember of that missing spark Sasha had mentioned? A mental fabrication to fill up that void inside him?

Even as he thought this, he felt the ember die out and his insides hollowed out again.

"Maybe you're right," he said, leaning back on the couch and throwing a hand over his eyes. "Jesus Christ, I feel like I'm cracking up. A head-shrinker might be exactly what I need."

"I'm not trying to pressure you. I merely wanted to bring it up as an option, something to consider."

"I'll take it under advisement. I wouldn't want to go to your therapist though, as I'm sure whoever it is has a full plate dealing with your big bag of nuts."

The joke was lame, but Sasha laughed anyway at the attempt. She glanced at her watch and grimaced. "I really do have to get to work."

"Go. I'm fine. I need to finish getting ready myself."

They stood, and Sasha gave him an awkward hug he stiffly returned. "I want you to go get a new cell phone and call me tonight. Promise."

"Deal."

After he saw her out, he leaned his forehead against the door. He felt like an idiot, getting his best friend over here to tell her he thought his apartment was haunted by Casper the Unfriendly Ghost, who had nothing better to do than knock things off shelves and cover his toiletries in bubble bath. It would be funny if it wasn't so pathetic.

He looked over at the oven clock. Even if he left right now, he'd still be late for work. He wasn't too worried about it though. He figured Zane would give him a lot of leeway for a while. Still, he needed to get his ass in gear and not push it. He could only play the poor-me card so long before it wore thin.

Still, before putting on his shoes and heading out, he went to the kitchen and rummaged through the junk drawer until he found the card for the psychologist.

7: Therapy

Berkley sat in the leather chair, fiddling with his new cell phone. A basic pre-pay thing. Nothing fancy, no bells or whistles. Minimally functional, Sasha had called it. He thought the phrase aptly described himself.

"Do you need to make a call?" Dr. Evans asked.

Berkley shook his head and stuffed the phone in his pocket. "Sorry."

The psychologist smiled from behind her desk. She didn't look anything like Berkley had been expecting. She was relatively young, no older than Berkley at least. No glasses, hair loose down her back instead of pulled into a tight librarian bun on top of her head. She had no notepad on her desk in which she'd scribble mysterious notes as he talked. However, the PhD framed on the wall behind her was from a reputable university.

"Let me ask the obvious question," she said. "Considering what happened in that apartment, why don't you move so you aren't faced with the constant reminder?"

"Going to have to plead poverty on this one, Doc. I can't afford a deposit on a new place right now. Hell, I can barely pay my rent as it is. If my health insurance from work wasn't covering this, I wouldn't be here now. It's actually kind of funny, I would watch old haunted house movies like *The Amityville Horror* and wonder why they didn't just get the hell out of Dodge. Now I know."

"Sometimes you're stuck with your ghosts," Dr. Evans said, leaning back in her chair.

"I was only making a comparison. I didn't mean literal ghosts or anything. I realize I may have gotten carried away for a minute thinking my apartment was haunted. I guess in psychological jargon, maybe that was just a symptom of a deeper issue or something. That's what

I'm here to figure out."

Dr. Evans smiled again. She did that a lot, and the smile was hard to read. "So you say you feel disconnected, detached from life? Tell me about that."

Berkley shifted in the chair, causing the leather to squeak like the passing of gas. He wanted to bring out his phone again simply to give his hands something to do other than beating an un-rhythmic staccato on his thighs. "It's everything, and nothing. I mean, I go to work and it's just something to do to pass the time until I'm not at work. I turn on the TV and it all seems so stupid. I try to read but the books don't hold my interest. My friend Sasha and I used to have an ease about our relationship, almost a telepathy like we knew what the other was thinking at all times. Now when I talk to her, it feels awkward and vaguely uncomfortable. I don't really want to go out, and absolutely nothing brings me any joy. Even the stuff I used to love to do, things I thought were so fun like going to live theater and hiking … it all seems meaningless to me now."

"Anhedonia," Dr. Evans said.

"Excuse me?"

"It's a term that means you no longer derive pleasure from things that once brought you pleasure. Also describes a lack of motivation and desire to even seek out pleasurable stimuli."

"Well, that's me in a nutshell."

"I know it's of little comfort to you, but it isn't all that uncommon. Especially for people who've had near death experiences. A common misconception is that coming so close to death will make a person appreciate life more, but in reality the opposite often proves true. A near death experience makes a person hyperaware of how fragile and tenuous life can be and can lead them to conclude that life is therefore insignificant."

"Sometimes I think I'm a zombie, and I do mean that literally. I mean, what is a zombie? It's someone who died then came back. That's me. Only difference is I don't have a hunger for human flesh, because I don't really have a hunger for anything anymore. I can't even say I'm depressed, because that would suggest *feeling*. And I feel nothing. I'm like a dead guy still wandering around. I'm a zombie."

Dr. Evans leaned forward, placing her hands on the desk. "Okay, I'm going to say something unexpected and maybe a little radical. That's fine."

"What's fine? Me being a zombie?"

"Exactly."

Berkley found himself wondering if her degree might be a fake. "So I should accept this as my new normal?"

"Not forever, but for now it's fine. In fact, it might be worrying if you were feeling any different. Don't put pressure on yourself or judge yourself. Simply allow yourself to be, and we'll work on getting you past this George Romero phase of your recovery."

"How do I do that?" Berkley asked, leaning forward himself so that his elbows rested on his knees. He couldn't say he felt anything akin to excitement or hope, but he was eager to move beyond this sense of non-being and become a full-fledged person again. "How do I get past it?"

"Ever heard the expression, 'fake it 'til you make it'?"

"Yeah, had a similar thought myself recently, though that hardly sounds like a psychological term."

"Let's say it's a legitimate therapeutic concept broken down into a layman's catchphrase. If you want to regain your old passion and vigor, it's not going to merely come back to you. You have to chase after it. I realize that will be difficult to do with your current lack of motivation, but you will have to force yourself. Go see a play at the Chapman Culture Center, go hike Paris Mountain, even if you don't want to. Because I know you want to want to. So make yourself go do the things you used to enjoy. You're likely not going to enjoy them now, may even feel painful, but if you do it enough then it will become habit, routine. And eventually, I promise you the enjoyment will start to come back. First the pain then the routine and then the enjoyment."

Berkley sat back again, creating another of those flatulence squeaks. "I don't know, Doc."

Dr. Evans spread her hands wide. "What do you have to lose?"

Berkley laughed, and this one was almost genuine. As far as pep talks went, it wasn't exactly the best, but she did have a point.

What *did* he have to lose?

*

When Berkley walked into his apartment, the first thing he heard was running water. He hurried to the kitchen area, tossing his keys and cell onto the end of the bar. He found the faucet expelling water at full blast into the sink. He quickly turned off the flow, but still the sound of water continued. Now from the bathroom.

The tub. Hot water gushing, fogging up the room like the set of some cheap horror movie from the 50s. Dropping to his knees, heedless of the puddle that dampened his pants, he grabbed the handle and twisted. Placing his hands on the rim of the tub, he pushed himself up. As he turned for the door, his gaze fell on the mirror, partially obscured with condensation from the steam, and he paused, a startled gasp escaping like air from a punctured tire.

In the steam, letters could be made out. Near the top left corner, a capital K and I; in the lower right corner, a capital E and L and the remnants of another letter that he couldn't quite decipher.

"This isn't my imagination," he muttered, rushing from the bathroom to grab his phone. This time he would snap a picture and offer Sasha irrefutable evidence.

But when he reached the bar, he found only his keys. He scanned the floor on either side of the bar in case his cell had slid off but came up empty. He was certain he had brought it inside, but nevertheless he returned to his car and checked. Nothing.

Back inside, the atmosphere in the apartment felt different. Nothing tangible like a cold spot or a heaviness. More like a static electricity that charged the very air. A feeling that he wasn't alone.

Okay, so maybe that was his imagination, but the water had definitely been turned on when he got home, and the letters had been drawn in the steam as if from a phantom finger. And now his cell had gone missing.

He stepped back into the bathroom, seeing that the steam had completely dissipated and the letters were no longer visible. They'd disappeared like a ghost. He knew he should be more afraid, and a certain fear did nibble at the corners of his mind, but mostly he felt curious. Of course, that hadn't worked out too well for the cat.

He considered messaging Sasha, but she wouldn't want to hear what he had to say, would be interested only in what Dr. Evans had said. In fact, even if he'd managed to get a photo, might she have suspected he drew the letters on the mirror himself, proof that he needed counseling more than ever?

Realizing he needed to pee, he lifted the toilet lid. He'd gotten his zipper halfway down when he glanced into the bowl and gasped again.

His cell phone rested in the water at the bottom of the basin.

8: Reaching Out

The four of them sat in a line down the bar, perched on rickety unpadded wooden stools Berkley had picked up from Goodwill that morning. Berkley sat at the end closest to the wall, Sasha next to him, then Zane, and finally Ernie at the far end. Four had seemed like a good number for this impromptu dinner party/game night, one person for each side of the board. His first thought had been to invite Ernie, Sasha, and Jeffrey, but Berkley had balked at the idea of spending an evening with Jeffrey in his house, so he'd contacted Zane instead.

Dinner so far had been a quiet affair, everyone adjusting constantly to try to find a less uncomfortable position on the stools. The meal itself Berkley had thrown together quickly, two boxes of Hamburger Helper Mac & Cheese. He'd added too much water, making the sauce a bit soupy, and when he realized he had no ground beef in the freezer, instead of running back to the Publix grocery store, he'd simply used some ground sausage that had been sitting in there for God knew how long. This gave the whole dish a surprising and not altogether pleasant flavor.

Of course, the dinner was merely a ruse, a convenient pretense to get everyone here. The real festivities would begin once everyone finished eating, and Berkley was eager to get to it.

Berkley jabbed a few pieces of macaroni with his fork, careful to eat around the questionable sausage chunks, and chewed on them. Tough and undercooked, not even tender enough to be called al dente. "Sorry," he said to the group after he swallowed. "I know the cuisine isn't exactly impressive."

Sasha, who had been pushing the mess around on her plate for the last couple of minutes without actually taking a bite, smiled. "No, it's … um, interesting. I've never had anything quite like it."

Berkley had called her last night after going out and buying yet another new cell phone. He hadn't wanted to spend any more money than necessary on his second replacement, and he'd found one of the old-fashioned flip-phones at Walgreens, seventy-five percent off its original price of thirty bucks. If the other had been minimally functional, this one was practically prehistoric but it got the job done.

Sasha had initially been absurdly excited about the invitation, probably seeing it as proof that a single counseling session had already born fruit, bringing Berkley back out of his shell. He hadn't doubted for a second that Ernie would accept the invitation, though Berkley did detect some disappointment when the older man realized it wasn't a quiet dinner for two. At first, Zane had seemed perplexed by their invitation, since they and Berkley had never spent any time together outside of work, a business relationship as opposed to a social one. Still, they had agreed. At this point, all three were likely regretting their choice to attend this sad little gathering.

"Yeah, it's fine," Zane said politely even as they pushed the plate away. "I'm not really all that hungry, though. Had a big lunch."

Ernie, meanwhile, had scoffed down half his helping. The expression on his face suggested this to be an unpleasant task, but still he shoveled another forkful into his mouth. The things people will do when they want to get into someone's pants, Berkley mused.

"Well," Berkley said, pushing his own plate away, "if we're done with dinner, what do you say we move on to the game portion of the night?"

Sasha hopped off her stool quickly, as if the Helper were toxic and she couldn't wait to distance herself from it. "Sounds good to me. As long as it's not Monopoly. I have work in the morning, and that's a game that last forever."

"I have Clue at my apartment," Ernie said. "I could run over and grab it."

"No need," Berkley said, already walking across the apartment. He'd taken four throw pillows and placed them around the coffee table, and now he squatted down and reached underneath the table to pull out the game he'd bought at Walmart this morning after leaving Goodwill. Standing, he turned toward his friends, holding the box up for them to see.

Sasha stopped mid-step. "That's a Ouija board."

"I know. I thought it would be some good spooky fun."

Ernie stood behind Sasha, almost looking as if he were using her as a human shield against the evil emanating from Berkley's hands. "Ouija's not a game," he said. "It can open doorways to demons and shit. I've seen documentaries on YouTube."

Berkley glanced down at the box. "It's made by Hasbro."

"Sounds like fun," Zane said, walking over and taking the box. "I've always wanted to try one of these."

Berkley smiled grateful at Zane, happy that he'd invited them.

Sasha came over as well, and after decades of friendship, he could read the complex emotion on her face. She knew the Ouija was an ambush, that he still had not let go of all this ghost nonsense, and she was royally pissed. Yet she would not make a scene in front of Ernie and Zane, but the next time she got him alone, he was going to catch almighty hell.

Zane had already opened the box, plopping down on one of the pillows and setting the board in the center of the table. Berkley took the pillow to Zane's right and Sasha sat directly across from Berkley. Ernie came last, more reluctantly than he'd eaten the disgusting meal, but he came nonetheless, completing the circle. Or the square, as it were.

"Okay," Zane said, taking the planchette and placing it on the board, "I assume we've all seen enough horror movies that we all know how this works. We all place our fingers lightly – very lightly – on the planchette."

"The what?" Ernie asked.

Zane held up the little triangular piece and sat it back down. "We place our fingers lightly on this, sort of empty and open our minds at the same time, invite any spirits in the vicinity to communicate with us only through the Ouija. That's an important part. We have to specify only through the Ouija. If we're lucky, a spirit will move the planchette across the board to spell out answers to whatever questions we ask. Once we're done, it's imperative that we move the planchette over each letter of the Goodbye at the bottom of the board. That will close the doorway to the spirits."

Berkley had never seen Zane quite this animated. He wondered if this was simply how they were outside of work, or was it specific to the task at hand?

"You seem to know a lot about this for someone who's never tried a Ouija before," Ernie said with a nervous laugh.

Zane shrugged. "I have an interest in the occult. Nothing serious, but I like to read about it. Fascinating subject."

"Is it too bright in here?" Berkley asked. "Should I turn off some of the lights, maybe get some candles?"

"I don't think that'll be necessary."

Berkley could sense Sasha giving him some major side-eye, but he rather pointedly ignored it. Whatever she thought, whatever Dr. Evans thought, he *knew* Kevin was haunting this apartment, and maybe acknowledging him and communicating with him would be the key to getting rid of him.

"Put the tips of your fingers on the planchette like this," Zane said, demonstrating with their own hands. "The key is to not press down on it but barely rest the tips against the plastic."

"Why do your fingers need to be on it at all?" Sasha asked, the sarcasm dripping heavy like rich cream. "I mean, why can't the spirit move the piece on its own without us touching it?"

Zane, missing the sarcasm or simply immune to it, seemed to give the question some actual thought before answering. "I think the theory is that it's hard for a disembodied spirit to cause physical phenomenon, but it can draw energy from the living. So if we're lightly touching the planchette, makes it easier for the spirit to manipulate it."

Berkley didn't miss Sasha's epic eye roll, but he didn't care. He only hoped her skepticism wouldn't prevent Kevin from manifesting or whatever.

Jesus, two weeks ago I would have been mocking this sort of mumbo-jumbo right alongside Sasha, and now I'm a diehard believer. Kind of crazy.

True, but one thing that had always bugged Berkley about that old TV show *The X-Files* was how long Scully, the skeptic, had remained a skeptic even in the light of compounding evidence. That took the idea of being rational to a level of stubbornness that was almost religious in its dismissal of facts. Crazy as it was, too much had happened in too short a time for Berkley to doubt.

"If we're going to do this, let's get it over with," Ernie said, placing his fingers on the planchette. Berkley followed suit, and finally Sasha.

They sat there on their pillows for a full minute, no one speaking until Ernie asked, "Have we started?"

Berkley looked to Zane, who had rapidly become the resident expert in Berkley's mind. "You seem to know the most about this sort of thing. Will you sort of lead us?"

The expression on Zane's face was one of pride and a certain seriousness that under other circumstances Berkley may have found amusing. "Okay," Zane said after clearing their throat, "like I said, try to sort of empty your mind and open yourself up to the other side."

Berkley didn't look over at Sasha, but he could practically *feel* another eye roll. Looking over at Ernie, his neighbor seemed shaken but he managed a smile, as if to say, *All in good fun ... right?*

"If there are any spirits here," Zane said, lifting their head to gaze at the ceiling as if that would be where all self-respecting ghosts would hang out, "I invite you to speak to us. Please use the Ouija board only. Are there any spirits with us in this apartment?"

This time, half a minute passed in silence.

"Guess no one's home," Sasha said with a laugh.

Zane shushed her. "Do you always answer your phone on the first ring? We need to give them time to answer."

Sasha opened her mouth, no doubt to voice a sarcastic retort, but then she looked across at Berkley and pressed her lips together. He detected some pity there, but mostly love. He had a feeling she wouldn't interrupt again, deciding to go through with this even though she thought it was ridiculous, if for no other reason than her best friend's peace of mind.

Zane gazed up at the ceiling again and said, "If there are any spirits here who have a message for us, we're receptive to hearing what you have to say. Use the Ouija to deliver that message."

As the seconds ticked by, Berkley began to feel silly and suspected nothing was going to happen … and then he realized his fingertips were tingling with a pins-and-needles sensation. Beneath his fingers, he thought he felt the planchette begin to vibrate. Such a subtle movement, he couldn't be sure.

He became sure when Sasha said, "Okay, who's doing that?"

Zane shushed her again, but less harshly this time. "I think they're trying to make contact."

The vibration increase until the planchette was clattering on the board. Berkley resisted the urge to snatch his hands away. All around the coffee table, his three friends wore identical open-mouthed looks of wonder and fear, but no one removed their fingers.

"Seriously, which one of you is doing this?" Sasha asked, but the tremor in her voice suggested she had started to become skeptical of her own skepticism.

"We know you are here," Zane said loudly. "Do you wish to communicate with us?"

Suddenly the planchette jerked out from beneath everyone's fingertips, sliding across the board to the upper left corner, stopping with the circle at its center perfectly placed above the word YES.

2B

9: The Answer

At first no one spoke. Or moved. Or even breathed, it seemed. Anticipation crackled in the air like the electric energy before a storm. Zane broke the spell by placing their fingers back on the planchette and saying, "Come on, guys. It's working."

Ernie shook his head and scooted back away from the coffee table. "I don't want to do this anymore."

Berkley felt a growing annoyance with Ernie, but before he could express it, Zane spoke up more magnanimously. "That's fine. You can sit this out if you want."

Ernie shot to his feet and bypassed the sofa, taking a seat on the edge of the bed. As if he wanted to put as much distance as possible between him and the board.

"Anyone else want to stop?" Zane asked.

Berkley answered by placing his fingers on the planchette next to Zane's. Sasha hesitated, looking from the Ouija to Ernie across the apartment to Berkley then back to the Ouija. After taking a deep breath, she also put her fingers on the planchette. She had never been one to shy away from a challenge, and he suspected that she was still trying to devise a rational explanation for the planchette moving on its own.

"Okay," Zane said. "We hear you, we acknowledge you. We're here to listen. Can you tell us your name?"

This time there was no pause or vibration; the planchette immediately started to move. First to the M then to the E.

Then it stopped.

"Me?" Sasha said. "That's very non-specific."

"I've read that spirits are notoriously bad spellers," Zane offered. "Maybe Mel? Or it could be initials. Can't be

Melissa Etheridge because she's not dead."

Berkley ignored the attempt at humor, a full-body chill encasing him like a sheet of ice. It took him three attempts to finally get his words out. "It's Kevin."

Zane frowned. "How do you figure?"

"Yeah," Sasha said. "Even if Kevin is a lousy speller, ME is pretty bad."

"It's this lame joke he had. He would say 'Knock Knock' and when I'd ask 'Who's there?' he'd laugh and answer, 'Me. I'm standing right in front of you.'"

"That's a bit of a stretch, sweetie," Sasha said in a gentle voice. A pitying voice.

"I'm telling you, it's Kevin. He's still here."

Zane looked uncertain for the first time, the real import of this little Ouija session apparently just hitting them. "Maybe that's enough for tonight."

"No," Berkley said, placing his fingertips on the planchette again. "Kevin, is that you? Tell them it's you."

The planchette began to move again, and Berkley lifted his fingers. The plastic triangle continued to slide around the board of its own volition. Zane read out the eight letters as they were highlighted.

"K. I. L. M. Y. S. E. F."

"Kill myself, see?" Berkley said, his voice thrumming with excitement. "He killed himself in my bathroom. It's him."

Sasha stood and took a step away from the coffee table. "I'm done."

"I should really get going," Ernie said, though he didn't move from his place on the bed.

"Fine," Berkley shouted. "Both of you can get lost. Zane and I will do this ourselves."

But one look at Zane's face told Berkley that he was

in this alone.

"I'm so sorry," Zane said. "I wasn't thinking. I should have been more sensitive to what you've been through and what happened here. This was a bad idea."

Berkley's frustration manifested in a roar and he slammed his fists down on the table, causing the board to jump. "Don't you all see? This is real. I'm not crazy, Kevin is haunting me. He's probably pissed that he didn't get to finish the job in his little murder/suicide plan. I need to get him to leave me alone. If you guys are too pussy to help me then I'll do it by myself."

He reached for the planchette again, but the plastic piece flew off the board, sailing over Berkley's shoulder to the kitchen, where it struck the fridge then clattered onto the worn linoleum. At the same instant, water began to pour from the kitchen sink faucet. The sound from the bathroom suggested the same had happened in the tub.

Sasha let out a scream when the closet door folded open with a bang, and clothes flung themselves out, hangers and all, to flutter and twist through the air. The refrigerator door also opened, banging against the counter, and all the groceries Sasha had stocked it with began to rain out onto the floor, a few glass jars shattering. The overhead light flared and brightened, a loud buzzing filling the air, before finally popping, the bulb inside the fixture shattering. The only light in the apartment now came from the fridge.

All of this transpired in a matter of seconds, but the lull that came after felt pregnant with the promise of more chaos to come. Silence except for everyone's harsh breathing. While it may have been only in his imagination, Berkley thought he detected five different breath sounds, one more than the number of people in the apartment.

Gradually he became aware of another sound, a sort of muffled knocking. He scanned the apartment, seeking the source, and realized that the Murphy bed was bouncing, lifting slightly then clomping back onto the carpeted floor. Ernie, in his stunned state, didn't seem to even notice though he still sat on the edge of the bed.

Realizing what was about to happen, Berkley rose from a crouch and bolted across the room. He grabbed Ernie by the arm and jerked him onto the floor an instant before the bed shot straight up, slamming into its cubby in the wall with enough force that the plaster to either side cracked, fine white dust sifting down like snow.

Ernie looked up at Berkley with wide, blank eyes. "You saved my life."

"I don't know about that," Berkley said, offering a hand to help Ernie to his feet. "Probably saved you from some broken bones though."

Sasha walked slowly across the apartment, making sure to avoid stepping directly on any of the clothing littering the floor as if afraid it may become animated again and tangle around her ankles. "You need to pack a bag."

"What?" Berkley said.

"There's no way I'm letting you stay here tonight. You're coming home with me, no arguments."

Berkley looked around at the mess and realized he had no arguments to make.

Zane tried to stand, plopped back onto the pillow, then tried again. "That really just happened," they said. "I mean, *really* really."

Sasha took Berkley's hand and squeezed. "I'm so sorry I didn't believe you. Under the circumstances it just seemed ... no, there's no excuse. I'm sorry."

"Don't worry about it. I had my own doubts, but

now we know for sure."

Berkley had expected to be more relieved at this confirmation of his suspicion and to have others believe him, as well as more afraid of the ramifications, and there had been a surge of those emotions, but already they were fading. Leaving him to feel adrift and empty again.

Perhaps this is how hopelessness feels.

"I don't want to be here," Ernie said, already sidling toward the door.

"None of us should be here," Sasha said. "Berkley, sweetie, grab what you need but make it snappy. We need to make tracks."

Zane cursed under their breath and suddenly rushed into the kitchen, kicking through the debris from the fridge, ducking out of sight behind the counter.

"What are you doing?" Berkley said.

Zane popped back into view, holding up the planchette. "We have to close the doorway before we go."

Back at the coffee table, Zane knelt down and placed the planchette on the Ouija board, sliding it methodically to each of the letters across the bottom.

G-O-O-D-B-Y-E

10: It Follows

Berkley sat on Sasha's sofa, listening to the screaming coming from the bedroom.

Actually, Sasha wasn't screaming. She tried to keep her voice low, quite in contrast to Jeffrey's histrionic shouting that surely could be heard by everyone in the complex. Certainly each word was clear to Berkley, like nails being driven into his ears.

"I don't want him here," Jeffrey said loudly, almost as if wanted Berkley to hear. Which he probably did.

Sasha's voice, while softer, was still audible. "Jeff, have a little compassion. He's having a rough time, and he needs his friends."

"He's an emotional cripple and a sponge. He's been sucking up all your energy for years. He has a crisis and you go running."

"Yes, and if I have a crisis, he comes running. That's what friends do."

"Friendships can be toxic, you know. He's toxic, why else would he have attracted a crazy nut like that?"

"Jesus, Jeff, keep your voice down."

"You're not my boss. I'll talk as loud as I want."

"This is my place, and I say to keep your voice down," Sasha said, her own voice rising sharply.

"*Your* place. I thought it was *our* place."

"Mine is the only name on the lease. You moved in with me, remember?"

"And I pay my fair share."

Sasha laughed, and it wasn't a pleasant sound. "You pay the water and electric. You think that compares with everything I shell out for the rent and groceries and cable and internet? Maybe this is a case of the mop calling the sponge absorbent."

"You knew when we met that I didn't make much money and you said that didn't matter, but now you're going to throw that back in my face?"

A half a minute passed before Sasha responded, and when she did her voice had become more calm and reasoned. "Look, I don't want to fight. *You* knew when we met that Berkley was my oldest friend and that he means a lot to me. I'm sorry if you consider it an inconvenience having him here, but he's going to be staying for a while."

"And exactly how long is a while?"

"As long as he needs to," she said, her voice still calm but full of steel. "At least until he finds another place he can afford. He's not going back to that apartment."

Jeffrey grumbled, his voice dipping so that Berkley couldn't make out the words.

Berkley felt drained and tired, as if he hadn't slept in a year. A dazed state came over him so that nothing seemed entirely real, as if this wasn't life but some movie where he'd lost the thread of the plot. Sasha's spacious one-bedroom apartment merely a set, and he an actor fuzzy on his lines and character motivation. He felt he'd been added to this scene in a rewrite but served no real purpose in it.

The bedroom door opened and Sasha stepped out, carrying a folded blanket and pillow in her arms. Behind her, Berkley caught a glimpse of Jeffrey, his face twisted into an ugly mask of anger and resentment, then he slammed the door.

Sasha took a seat next to Berkley, handing over the bedding, smiling as if the argument hadn't happened. "Hope the sofa isn't too lumpy."

"It'll be fine," Berkley said. "Sorry if I'm causing trouble in paradise."

Sasha gave one of her half-shrugs. "It's hardly ever what I'd call paradise around here. If we weren't yelling about you, we'd be yelling about him peeing on the toilet seat or leaving his beard trimmings in the sink."

Berkley knew he should offer his friend some sympathy for her relationship woes, but he honestly lacked the energy. Instead he said, "So you didn't tell him about what happened at my apartment?"

"No, just that you're having trouble dealing with everything and needed to be away from there. That's all he needs to know."

"Pretty scary stuff, huh?"

Sasha's mouth tightened and her posture stiffened. "I don't know what to think."

"You're not doubting what we experienced, are you?"

She shook her head. "I wish I could doubt it, but I was there. I was in the thick of it. I don't know how it's possible or what it all means though."

"Seems clear enough to me. Kevin wants to finish what he started."

"I meant it when I said me casa is su casa for as long as it takes to find you a new apartment."

"I appreciate that."

Sasha stood and said, "I'm going to turn in. If you aren't tired, feel free to watch TV as long as you keep the volume low. You know where the bathroom is, and help yourself to anything in the fridge if you want a snack."

Berkley stared through the archway across the room into the tidy kitchen. He found himself flashing on all the items in his own fridge throwing themselves off the shelves like lemmings over a cliff, and bile churned in his stomach. "I think I'm good, but thanks."

"Okay, I'll see you in the morning."

After Sasha retired to the bedroom, where he figured she and Jeffrey would sleep on opposite ends of the bed with their backs to each other, Berkley picked up the remote and considered flipping through the channels, but in the end, he turned off the light and stretched out on the sofa. He figured sleep would be an impossible goal, but exhaustion overcame him within minutes and he drifted off.

*

Berkley awoke to the sound of doors slamming. At first he thought Sasha and Jeffrey must be having some kind of epic middle-of-the-night argument of apocalyptic proportions, but he heard no screaming and the slamming continued unabated. It sounded as if the entire cast of that old Stomp theater group had invaded the apartment.

Pushing up on one elbow, Berkley fumbled for the lamp on the end table next to the sofa, nearly toppled it, then got the light on. The cacophony came from the kitchen, and through the archway he could see all the cabinet doors above the sink flying open and banging shut again, one after the other, over and over.

"What the fuck are you doing out here?" Jeffrey shouted, busting out of the bedroom in only a pair of boxers. Sasha stumbled along behind him, wearing an oversized t-shirt as a nightgown.

Jeffrey spotted his unwanted houseguest still on the sofa and then his eyes turned to the kitchen, where the cabinets continued their applause break. Anger turned to confusion then to fear all in the duration of half a second. Sasha put a hand to her mouth and muffled a scream.

The faucet of the kitchen sink tore loose and hurtled through the air like a Chinese throwing star, water geysering up in a violent spray to douse the kitchen in a downpour. Plates cascaded out of the cabinets, shattering on the counter and floor. The oven door began to open and close like a gaping mouth. The bedroom door also slammed shut, causing both Sasha and Jeffrey to scream this time.

Then as suddenly as it all began, it ended. Even the water shooting from the broken faucet receded to a dribble. The silence that followed felt large and oppressive, as if it had substance.

"What's going on here?" Jeffrey asked in a squeaky voice, and Berkley realized that a dark wet spot had formed at the crotch of his boxers.

Berkley didn't answer, instead only found himself thinking of the shredded book at Page to Page. Of course, how could he have been so foolish as to not recognize the significance of that?

Sasha also didn't answer Jeffrey, pushing past him to come to Berkley's side. "Are you okay?" she asked.

Berkley stared at her blankly for a moment before finding his voice. "It's not the apartment. It's *me*. Kevin's ghost is attached to me somehow. The apartment isn't haunted; I am."

"Haunted?" Jeffrey said. "Ghost? Somebody tell me what the hell is happening."

Berkley stood and pulled away from Sasha. "I should go."

"Yes, definitely, you should go," Jeffrey said. "I don't know what to make of this, but if you brought it here then I want you gone."

"Shut up, Jeff. Berkley isn't going anywhere."

Those were her words, but Berkley could tell by her expression that she too would be more at ease if he were not here right now. He felt no sting at this. Hell, under the circumstances he couldn't exactly blame her.

"I have to go. Sasha, it isn't safe for me to stay. This is my problem to deal with, not yours."

"We're best friends. Your problems *are* my problems."

"We're not talking about a traffic ticket I can't pay or an annoying coworker I need to vent about. This is some seriously freaky shit, and it's not fair for me to bring it into your place."

"For Christ's sake, let him go," Jeffrey growled, cupping his hands in front of his crotch as if just noticing he'd pissed himself.

Sasha shot Jeffrey a poisonous glare but then looked back at Berkley with resignation in her eyes. "If you're going to leave, don't go back to your apartment. Get a motel room."

"Doesn't matter where I go, Kevin will follow me. A motel room is no safer than my apartment."

"We don't know that. We don't know anything about any of this really. The apartment is where he died, so maybe he's stronger there or something."

"He seemed pretty strong here," Berkley said, gesturing toward the kitchen.

Jeffrey turned without warning and bolted into the bedroom. When he returned, he had changed into different boxers and held his wallet, pulling cash from it. "Here," he said, shoving the bills into Berkley's hand. "If it's a cost issue, the motel room is on me."

Berkley almost felt like laughing. He knew it must be serious if Jeffrey was willingly offering his own money.

Sasha squeezed Berkley's shoulder. "Please sweetie, for my own peace of mind, don't go back to the apartment."

Berkley realized this was a guilt thing. Sasha didn't

want him here, because of the baggage he brought along with him (and could that be Kevin's plan, to isolate him?), and she felt shitty about that. To ease her conscience, she needed to feel she was doing something to help keep her friend out of danger, even if the gesture was empty.

"Fine," he said, wadding the money up in his fist. "I'll get a room."

He had brought only a duffle bag of stuff with him and hadn't unpacked anything but his toothbrush, so he was ready to go within minutes, still wearing the sweats he slept in and a pair of ratty sneakers.

Jeffrey didn't bother with a goodbye, retreating to the bedroom without a word, but Sasha hugged him for an uncomfortably long time and made him promise to call her in the morning. Then she too disappeared into the bedroom.

As Berkley slipped out the door, he tossed the cash Jeffrey had given him onto the entry table.

11: Psychosexual

Berkley stood outside his apartment door staring at the crooked B for several minutes. The outside light, housed in the cracked glass shade, turned on then began to flicker and stutter before going out again.

Of course Berkley hadn't gone to a motel. This wasn't a problem he could run from; this was a problem that he had to face. Here was where it all began, and if he hoped to find a way to end it, here was where that would have to take place as well. He couldn't know that for sure, but he felt it in his gut. An instinct or intuition.

He unlocked the door and let himself in, flipping the light switch before remembering the overhead had burst during the melee earlier. Kicking the door closed with a foot, he crossed the apartment and turned on the floor lamp. He turned and looked at the Ouija still laid out on the coffee table. Some might think he should fear it or experience an emanation of malice from it, but no. It was merely a game, a toy. The board bore no responsibility for what had happened here.

Kevin had needed no invitation to break into the apartment and drown Kevin in the tub. In death, he certainly needed even less of an invitation.

Berkley scanned the devastation of the apartment. The kitchen was a disaster, and clothes still littered the floor as if a group of people with questionable fashion sense had all been raptured right out of their outfits. At some point since he'd left with Sasha, the bed had fallen back out of the wall, the bedclothes rumbled and messy.

In the bathroom, he showed no surprise to find that the tub had been plugged and filled with water. As he watched, the water began to lap at the sides of the tub, undulating slightly as if beckoning him to step inside, to submerge himself, to allow Kevin's work to be completed.

A knocking startled Berkley out of his reverie. No phantom knocking, this, but a rapping at his front door.

He opened up to find Ernie waiting in a pajama set with little sailboats all over it, something that seemed designed for little kids though obviously made in grown-men sizes.

"I heard noises over here," Ernie said. "At first I thought it was … well, you know. Then I looked out and saw your car was back."

"Sorry if I woke you."

"Hell, I wasn't sleeping. I doubt I'll be sleeping much for the next few months."

"Then I'm sorry for that. This is all my fault."

"Berk, no," Ernie said, taking a step toward the doorway then stopping abruptly. Like a vampire not able to cross the threshold. "You shouldn't blame yourself for any of this."

"It's hard not to. It's like I'm cursed or something."

"How come you're back?" Ernie asked. "I thought you were staying with Sasha."

Berkley gave him a quick rundown of the events that transpired at Sasha's.

"Oh, that's horrible," Ernie said, and this time he overcame his fear and stepped into the doorway, wrapping his arms around Berkley.

Berkley allowed the embrace, even if he didn't return it. While he couldn't blame Sasha for turning him out, he had to admit it felt like a rejection of sorts. At least here was someone still willing to be near him, to touch him, to risk being tainted by Berkley's aforementioned curse.

When Ernie pulled back, he maintained a grip on Berkley's forearms. "Is there anything I can do for you?"

Berkley shook his head. "I don't think there's anything anyone can do for me."

"I want to apologize for earlier tonight. I know I freaked out a bit, but you have to understand I've never believed in anything remotely supernatural. Hell, I don't even believe in women's intuition. It's kind of like a hardcore atheist meeting God face to face or something. Messed with my worldview, I guess you could say."

"Tell me about it. I feel like my life has become an episode of *Stranger Things*. And I'm Barbara."

"Justice for Barb," Ernie said with a laugh. He then glanced past Berkley, into the gloomy apartment. "I worry about you being here. What if something happens?"

"If something's going to happen then it's going to happen, no matter where I am."

"Why don't you come stay at my apartment? You can have the bed; I'll take the couch. You just shouldn't be alone right now."

Berkley certainly didn't want to stay at Ernie's apartment – the few times he'd been inside had convinced him the older man was a borderline hoarder, an already cramped space becoming downright claustrophobic with all the junk piled up like giant Jenga towers – but he had to admit that he also didn't want to be alone. He didn't want conversation or even companionship necessarily, but he yearned for another warm living body next to him for comfort. To anchor him, remind him that he too was still a warm living body, that he hadn't died in that bathtub. Or at least hadn't stayed dead. Who better to remind him of that than the man who'd brought him back from the clutches of Death?

"Why don't you stay in my apartment tonight?" Berkley asked, hesitating only a second before adding, "We can share the bed."

Ernie's mouth dropped open, and Berkley could see the debate going on in the man's eyes as he tried to figure out if Berkley's invitation was innocuous or more seductive. To cast away all ambiguity, Berkley reached out and cupped Ernie's crotch, squeezing the bulge.

"Stay with me," Berkley said in a thin, breathy voice.

Ernie glanced into the apartment again, no doubt remembering what had taken place there earlier, but the stiffening in his pajama pants suggested his brain wouldn't be in control of his thought processes much longer. When Berkley backed up into the apartment, Ernie followed.

Ernie closed the door behind him then dove in for a kiss, but Berkley ducked his head to the side and began to nibble on his neighbor's earlobe, even as his hands slid up under Ernie's top to give his nipples light and teasing tweaks.

"God, you have no idea how long I've wanted this," Ernie said between panting breaths. "So many nights lying in bed right next door, fantasizing about it, but I didn't think you were interested in – *ow!*"

Berkley realized his nibbling had become biting, and his playful tweaks had become painful pinches. He pulled Ernie's shirt off in one smooth fluid motion then practically dragged the man to the bed, tossing him down so that Ernie landed on his back. Removing his own shirt, Berkley climbed onto the bed, straddling Ernie then leaning his head down to lick and suck the man's nipples. Ernie arched his back and moaned deep in his throat, placing a hand on the back of Berkley's head.

Berkley allowed his mouth and tongue to stray lower, leaving a sticky trail down Ernie's chest and stomach. He slid the man's pajama pants down so that he could envelop him.

Ernie hissed as if being scaled. "I can't believe this is happening."

After using his mouth for several minutes, Berkley came up for air and quickly yanked Ernie's pants all the way off. Berkley then removed his own, straddled his neighbor again, then reached over to the bedside table, opening the drawer and pulling out a foil-wrapped condom. "I want you inside me," he said then tore the packet open with his teeth.

Ernie looked uncertain. "I'm really more of a bottom my – "

Berkley silenced him with a finger to his lips. "Not tonight."

Berkley rolled the condom onto Ernie with practiced ease then positioned himself, pushing back. Ernie cried out, pulling at his own hair, and thrust his hips upward. Berkley planted his hands firmly on the man's chest and began to bounce, pulling forward then grinding back.

"Get on top," Berkley said after a while, grabbing Ernie by the shoulders and rolling them over.

Ernie leaned up on his elbows and tried again for a kiss, but Berkley turned his face to the side. "Harder," he gasped. "Go harder. Really make me feel it."

"I don't want to hurt you."

"Don't be a pussy. I said, *harder*!"

Ernie actually slowed his pace. "I'm not really comfortable in, you know, this role."

Berkley slapped Ernie in the face. He didn't even realize he was going to do it until his hand made contact. "Hurt me, you pansy! I want you to. Make me feel something, make me feel *anything*!"

Ernie pulled away, scrambling off the bed. He stood there, naked and shivering, before retrieving his pajama pants and hastily putting them on. "I know things are crazy right now, Berk, and I want to be there for you, but not like this. I can't give you what you need."

"Then get the fuck out!" Berkley yelled. He jumped out of bed, snatched up Ernie's shirt and tossed it in the man's face. "What good are you anyway? Can't give me what I need? I'll shout an Amen to that one!"

The stamp of hurt on Ernie's face was profound, but he shuffled quietly toward the door. As he opened it, he turned back and said, "If you need to talk – just *talk* – you know where to find me."

Berkley rushed forward, shoved Ernie out the door then slammed it. He stayed there for several minutes, staring at the flaking paint of the backside of the door, until his heartbeat slowed and his breathing evened out. What had come over him? He'd never been into rough sex before, and the way he had treated Ernie appalled him. As if it had been someone else in the driver's seat and not himself.

Could that be it? Was Kevin doing more than haunting Berkley? Could he also be possessing him in some way? Might that not explain why he felt so hollow and empty inside, not himself?

Berkley screamed when something hit him in the back. He turned and looked down to find the copy of *Mrs. Dalloway* lying at his feet. As he looked up and across the apartment toward his bookcase, another book flew off the shelves and pelted him right in the center of the chest. Several more paperbacks followed but Berkley swatted them aside like pesky flies.

"That all you got?" he screamed. "You'll have to do better than that, Kevin! Your Casper bit is getting old, and I will find a way to get rid of you. I swear to God, whatever it takes, I will get rid of you once and for all."

12: The Puddle

It felt surreal being at work considering the tumult his life had become. In haunted house movies, the characters' lives seemed to revolve solely around the ghostly encounters; rarely did you see extended scenes of them going about mundane, routine daily tasks. But this wasn't a movie. It was real life, and as the saying went, life had to go on.

As Berkley changed out the Bestsellers display at the front of the store, he glanced over at Annette behind the counter and felt a thread of bitterness twist in his chest. Before all this, whenever Berkley and Annette worked together, Zane always put Berkley on register. Zane had confided once that he too found Annette's chirpy voice annoying and figured it might annoy the customers as well.

Yet there she was, and here Berkley was, almost as if Zane wanted to limit Berkley's direct contact with the public. Zane didn't seem to want to have much direct contact with Berkley either; they had been squirreled away in the office almost since Berkley's shift had started.

I'm just being overly sensitive, seeing everything as a personal slight.

Berkley told himself that, but he wasn't sure he believed it.

"Hey Berkley, can you come here a sec?" Annette called. Since every statement she made sounded like a question, when she asked something in the form of an actual question, it always took Berkley's mind a moment to adjust.

He walked over to the counter, where a female customer with a side bun stood waiting.

"This lady wants to know if we have any Ron Rash poetry collections," Annette explained. "She said she didn't see any in the Poetry section, and you know the inventory better than me."

"Um, yeah. I think there are some over in the Southern Writers section," Berkley said, pointing to a bookcase right next to the entrance into the café.

The woman thanked him then left to peruse. Berkley started to walk away himself but Annette asked, "You doing okay?"

Berkley paused. How much did Annette know? Surely Zane wouldn't have mentioned the Ouija disaster, and he didn't think she even knew about what had gone down with Kevin. The news reports had kept Berkley's name out of it, and Zane wasn't one to share personal information about their staff. Gossip was strictly verboten at Page to Page.

"Not sleeping?" Annette asked when Berkley didn't answer right away.

"How did you know?"

"Bags under your eyes. Plus you've been working on Bestsellers for nearly an hour, and you normally knock that kind of stuff out in fifteen minutes flat."

Berkley had always considered Annette something of a self-absorbed kid, but maybe she was a little more cognizant of other people than he'd given her credit for. "Yeah, well, I'm having some issues in my personal life that make sleep a little difficult at the moment."

"You should try some yoga stretches before bed. I know that sounds all New-Agey, but I'm not suggesting crystals or chanting or anything. I'm taking this online Anatomy and Physiology course for fun, and I learned that forward bends in particular activate the parasympathetic nervous system which helps calm and relax you. It's not airy-fairy hooey but actual science."

This was by far the longest conversation Berkley had ever had with Annette, and he found himself irritated at discovering this new side of her. His life was too complicated as it was; he didn't have room to see her in anything other than one-dimensional terms.

"I'll have to give that a go," Berkley said, not even attempting to sound like he meant it.

Annette seemed not to notice his tone, or chose to ignore it. "I can recommend some online videos if you – "

"Hey, what the hell happened here?"

Berkley and Annette both turned to look toward the voice, a male customer standing near the front. Right next to the Bestsellers. Berkley walked over, and Annette came out from behind the counter to follow.

The first thing Berkley noticed was the large puddle around the rack that held the Bestsellers display, but it wasn't until Annette said, "Oh no, they're all ruined," that he realized the books themselves had been drenched. Already several of them bloated, their pages fanning out like the bellows of an accordion.

As if some Spidey-sense had been triggered, Zane picked that moment to come out of the back. "What's going on?" they asked when they noticed the little gathering.

Berkley found himself at a loss for words, so he let Annette answer.

"Someone poured water all over the Bestsellers. I don't know what happened. Berkley had been over here changing out the display."

He knew she hadn't meant that as an accusation, but it felt like one anyway.

"Doubt you'll be selling any of those," the customer said with a laugh. When no one else joined in, his laughter tapered and he wandered off.

Zane put their hands on their hips and surveyed the damage. They then tilted their head back to stare up at the ceiling, no doubt searching for a leak of some kind. "I don't know how I'm going to explain this to Jimmy and Brenda."

Jimmy and Brenda McNamara were the owners of Page to Page, and though they liked to project an image of aging hippies who opened the store out of nothing but their love of literature, Berkley knew they were real hard-asses when it came to the financial bottom line.

Annette stuck her toe in the puddle. "The water looks kind of sudsy, like it has detergent in it or … "

"Bubbles," Berkley finished.

Zane's gaze shot to Berkley, and their eyes locked in a shared understanding so total it was almost telepathic.

"Annette," Zane said, "would you mind running into the café and grabbing the mop out of the storage closet? Do your best to get up as much of the water as you can, and I'll be back in a few to deal with the books. Berkley, can I see you in my office please?"

Berkley followed Zane back through the store with his head down, feeling like a kid on his way to the principal's office to be punished, possibly expelled. Once inside the office with the door closed, Zane at first said nothing, simply paced around, thrumming with a nervous energy that made the air practically thrum with tension.

"This is part of it, isn't it?" Zane finally said. "Some kind of manifestation or whatever?"

"I think so."

"Jesus! Maybe the Ouija board was a mistake. I thought I closed the door last night."

"The Ouija isn't the door. I am."

Zane stopped, perching on the edge of their desk. "Sasha told me about what happened at her apartment last night. She was pretty freaked out."

"Yeah, it was – hey, wait a minute! You and Sasha *talk*?"

Sounded like a silly question, but Sasha and Zane occupied two very different spheres of his life, and it had never occurred to Berkley that the two would have any direct communication outside his presence.

"We text a little," Zane said, sounding oddly defensive. "Ever since … well, she was the one that came to the store and told me what had happened to you when you were in the hospital. We exchanged numbers and have kept in touch. Anyway, the point is I think it might be better if you left for the day, before anything else happens. Something more serious and even harder to explain."

Being turned out again. Understandable but it hurt nonetheless. Berkley was beginning to feel like a pariah. Still, this might work in his favor. He couldn't keep his mind on his work anyway, and there was something he had been contemplating doing today. This would afford him the perfect opportunity to do it.

"I guess you're right," he said. "Before I go, can I ask you a favor?"

Zane straightened up eagerly, looking as if they'd promise their firstborn if it would get Berkley out of the store quickly. "Name it."

"You said you're into all this occult stuff, right?"

"In an academic sense."

"Well, do you think you might know anyone who could help me with my situation?"

"Help? What do you mean exactly?"

"I don't know what I mean. I don't know much about any of this stuff. I just want Kevin gone. Do you know anyone who might be able to accomplish that? I don't care how. If they have to sacrifice live sheep in the middle of my apartment, I'm in as long as it works. I can't keep living like this."

Zane thought for a moment then lifted their right shoulder in a half-shrug, as if they had picked up Sasha's mannerisms through their new-found text friendship. "I don't know anyone personally, but I am a member of a few Facebook groups dedicated to the paranormal. I can ask around, see what I can find."

"I'd be forever grateful."

"Okay, I'll get right on it."

Berkley didn't waste any more time. He left the store, tossing a wave toward Annette as she mopped up the water, and headed to the parking garage a few blocks away. He hurried down the sidewalk with purposeful strides, a man on a mission.

Last night he had begun to think the key to beating Kevin might be to learn more about him, the man he'd been in life. Berkley had been surprised to realize how little he knew about the person he'd dated for several months. He did remember Kevin complaining about some ex whom he said never understood or appreciated him, but the only specific information Berkley could recall was that the guy's first name was Stan and he worked (or at least used to) as a receptionist at a pet grooming company on the west side of the city near the mall. One of those nauseatingly cutesy names.

Beauty for the Beasts.

When Berkley pulled out of the parking garage, he turned onto Highway 29 and headed west.

13: The Ex

When Berkley walked through the door, setting off a chime that sounded like barking dogs, the young man behind the front desk looked up, professional smile already in place. "Good morning. Welcome to Beauty for the Beasts."

Taking a closer look, Berkley realized the man wasn't as young as he'd first appeared. The frosted hair and synthetically-tanned skin couldn't quite mask the hair receding at the temples or the lines that crinkled the corners of his eyes and mouth. The guy was nearing the threshold of forty, if he hadn't already cleared the door. He wore no helpful nametag.

When Berkley didn't respond, merely stood there scrutinizing the receptionist, the man's eyes narrowed though his manufactured smile did not falter. "Doesn't look like you have a furry friend with you. Sorry, we don't groom humans, cutie."

Berkley realized he'd shown up with no real plan for what to say once he got here, so he blurted, "Are you Stan?"

The professional smile turned off instantly like someone had flipped a switch. "Do I know you?"

"Um, no, but we had a mutual acquaintance. Kevin Sparks."

Berkley didn't think he imagined the look of fear that twisted Stan's features before the man regained his composure. "How did you know Kevin?"

"We were dating. He … well, it was at my apartment … I'm the one he … "

"It was you," Kevin said. "Oh God, okay. Look, we can't talk in here but I'm due for a break. Go outside, around to the right side of the building, and I'll meet you in a few minutes. Is that good?"

Berkley nodded and went back outside. The day was overcast, a thick layer of mottled clouds blotting out the sky, but so far the rain had held off. He made his way to the narrow alley that separated Beauty for the Beasts from the dental building next door. The predominant feature of the alley was the large dumpster at the far end, and the smell that emanated from it caused Berkley to wrinkle his nose and turn his back to it, as if to rebuff the stench's advances.

As he waited, he wondered what he hoped to accomplish from this confab with Kevin's ex. He figured it could be summed up with that old cliché, "I don't know what I'm looking for, but I'll know when I find it." He didn't know what kind of information about Kevin might be useful, so gathering as much as he could and sifting through it seemed the best course of action. Another old cliché came to mind, "Knowledge is power."

A door at the back of the building, near the reeking dumpster, opened and Stan stepped out. He seemed unbothered by the smell, perhaps used to it. He pulled out a pack of cigarettes, lit one then held out the pack. Berkley declined the offer. He normally hated the smell of cigarette smoke, but it beat the stink of the dumpster so he welcomed the masking aroma.

Stan took a long drag, blew the smoke up toward the clouds, then said, "So you're the one Kevin tried to kill, huh?"

"He did kill me. Technically, I mean. My neighbor resuscitated me."

"I heard about it. They didn't use your name so I didn't know who you were, and to be honest I didn't give it much thought. I was just happy to know the bastard was dead and gone."

"Dead at least," Berkley muttered under his breath.

"How'd you know who I was? Did Kevin talk about me?"

"Some. Not exactly in the most flattering of terms."

"Did he tell you I dumped his ass and got a restraining order against him? Which he violated twice and had to spend a little bit of time in jail, though not enough for my taste."

Berkley shook his head. "Actually he told me that he broke up with you. Said you didn't understand him and didn't appreciate him."

Stan laughed, belching out smoke like a dragon with a busted furnace in its belly. "That's true enough, I suppose. I didn't understand how he could be such a schizo and I didn't appreciate him beating up on me the way he did."

"So he was abusive?"

"Hell yeah. Frankly, looking back I don't know why I put up with it as long as I did. All my life I kind of judged people who stayed with abusive partners, wondering why the hell they didn't just pack up and get lost. But when it happened to me, I found myself making excuses for him. My thinking was so twisted I even sort of thought it was my fault. The brain is a freaky thing, the rationalizations it can make. Anyway, I finally came to my senses when he cracked some ribs. I knew I needed to get out before he did some more serious damage. Like I said, even after the restraining order he kept harassing me for a while. Then one day he just dropped off the radar. At first, that made me nervous and I worried it was the calm before the storm. Then I felt relieved, figuring he must have found a new victim. I guess that would have been you."

"I broke it off after the first time he hit me."

"Smarter than I was. Although, considering how things turned out in the end, maybe not. Maybe you broke it off too soon, and that only made him more determined to go after you. Who knows how a brain that warped works."

"He certainly had some abandonment issues," Berkley said, thinking that he sounded a bit like Dr. Evans.

Stan laughed again. "That's an understatement. I mean, it's no wonder with the upbringing he had. Have you talked to his sister?"

Berkley felt like he'd been hit over the head with a baseball bat. "Wait, what? Kevin has a sister?"

Stan laughed again. "Yeah, we'd been dating quite a while before I found out myself. And then only because she showed up at his apartment one day while I was there. After she left, I confronted Kevin about keeping so much of his life from me. It escalated into a huge argument, and that was actually the first time he hit me. Should have said sayonara right then and there, but immediately he started blubbering and telling me how sorry he was, and how much it hurt him that I didn't trust him or believe in him, blah blah blah. I can't explain it, but by the time he got done with his 'apology,' he had me convinced I'd been the one who'd done something wrong. Pathetic, I know."

"Some people are just master manipulators," Berkley said.

"Or maybe some of us are just masters of gullibility. In any case, I did get very curious about his sister and his family. I found her on Instagram and sent her a message. We ended up getting together and she gave me all the dirt on the fucked-up upbringing she and Kevin had. Of course, I never let Kevin know I was in communication with her, and I made her swear she'd never tell him. As far as I know, she kept her promise."

"What did she tell you? What was so fucked up about their childhoods?"

Stan took one final deep drag then let the butt drop to the pavement, grinding it beneath the toe of his shoe. "That's not my dirt to spill."

"Come on, man. You've got to tell me. I need to know."

"Why?" Stan asked. "I know what he did to you was terrible, but the sick bastard is dead now. He can't hurt either one of us anymore."

Berkley felt the truth pushing at the back of his teeth, but he swallowed it back down. If he started talking about ghosts and hauntings, Stan would no doubt think he was nothing more than a kook in need of a padded room. Instead, Berkley told as much of the truth as he could without getting into all the supernatural stuff. "There's so much I need to understand. I'm not going to be able to get on with my life until I do."

Stan put his hands in his pockets and stared down at his shoes, causing his chin to balloon out like one of those Spring peeper frogs. The bitchy part of Berkley wanted to suggest that if Stan still wanted to pull off the illusion of youth, he should never look down, but insults rarely won people's confidence.

"Her name is Kaitlin," Stan said, glancing up again. "You can find her on Instagram just like I did. KSparks, that's her name on there."

"Okay, thanks. Are you sure you can't just tell me what you found out from her, save me the trouble?"

Stan shook his head. "I don't want to talk about this anymore. I've worked hard to put the whole disaster that was my relationship with Kevin behind me, but the wounds are still fresh. I know you have wounds of your own that go much deeper, but I can't rehash this, dredging up the past. I wish you luck on this journey, but this is my off-ramp."

Berkley could have continued to plead his case, but Stan's resolution seemed firm and unshakable. Berkley nodded, thanked him, then hurried back down the alley to the parking lot out front of the business. Rain began to spit down, the pregnant clouds finally giving birth to the promised storm.

As Berkley reached the corner of the building, Stan said from behind him, "Kevin must have really loved you, you know?"

Berkley stopped and turned back. "Why would you say something like that?"

Stan lit another cigarette, heedless of the drizzle, and took a couple of puffs before answering. "Well, he didn't kill himself over me."

14: Assisted Suicide

Berkley sat up on the sofa, his back resting against one of the arms and his legs stretched out over the cushions. He'd draped his blanket over him, and his pillow rested in his lap like a TV tray, his laptop on top of that. He knew he would be sleeping here again tonight, like a dad in a TV sitcom who had been banished to the sofa after a fight with the Mrs. Other than Berkley's disastrous tryst with Ernie, he had avoided the bed. He couldn't get the image of it slamming into the wall out of his mind.

On the laptop screen, another message from KSparks popped up. He'd made contact about half an hour ago, as he was sitting down to a nutritious meal of beef-flavored Ramen and an evening of intellectual stimulation in the form of *Designing Women* on YouTube. Now the 80s southern belles were forgotten, and the noodles were cold and congealed in a bowl on the coffee table.

So far KSpark's responses had been slow-coming and somewhat cagey. Berkley hadn't told her he was the one Kevin had tried to kill and in whose apartment the man had killed himself, afraid that would scare her off; instead, he'd simply said he had known her brother and wanted to find out more about what had led him to the actions at the end of his life. However, this wasn't getting him anywhere. She didn't seem to want to part with any real information.

Biting the bullet, Berkley typed, "Your brother drowned me in my own bathtub then blew his brains out all over my bathroom wall," then hit SEND.

A bit over-the-top and extreme, and he might find himself blocked, but he needed to get a reaction from her.

The minutes passed with excruciating slowness. Berkley glanced around the apartment, knowing he should be disgusted by the mess but not really feeling much of anything. He hadn't picked up any of the clothes strewn about, and though he'd made a half-assed attempt at cleaning the kitchen, the floor was still streaked with crusty bits of food and condiments. Ever since this whole nightmare had begun, the apartment no longer felt like his home; he felt like the ghost invading an unfamiliar domain. Why would he take the time to scrub a place that wasn't even his?

On the message screen, the little ellipsis appeared, indicating that KSparks was typing a new message. Berkley leaned forward, putting his face into the glow from the screen. Of course, she could be typing a message telling him to fuck off, but those three flickering dots caused a surge of hope.

Finally the message came through: "Can you meet for coffee tomorrow afternoon @ 2?"

Berkley responded with a "Yes" immediately. He was scheduled to work tomorrow, but he had a feeling Zane wouldn't mind if he took another day off.

She suggested Bella Latte, a trendy little independent coffee place frequented by hipsters too cool for the conglomerate Starbucks. Same kind of clientele that shunned Barnes & Noble for Page to Page. Berkley agreed and thanked her. She didn't respond, but at least the meeting had been set.

The laptop still open, he placed it on the coffee table between the bowl and his cell phone. The cell phone with four voicemail messages from Sasha he still hadn't listened to. He wasn't sure why he didn't answer or return her calls. Perhaps to punish her for wanting him out of her apartment. Illogical, since it had been his idea to leave in the first place, but pettiness often defied logic. Or maybe he knew her concern would only bring him down. For the first time in ages, he was feeling something almost akin to happiness. Silly, as he hadn't really accomplished anything yet, but it felt good to be taking any proactive steps at all. Plus he thought he might be on the right path, uncovering Kevin's secrets to use against him.

Outside the rain continued to fall, a rhythmic staccato that soothed him like a lullaby. It was only seven p.m., but his eyelids felt weighted. Not surprising, as he had gotten very little sleep the last several nights. He considered taking the bowl to the kitchen, dumping the noodles in the trash, but he didn't have the energy.

Instead he scooted further down the sofa, placing the pillow beneath his head, and turned on his side. Within minutes, he was asleep.

*

Berkley wasn't sure what woke him, the scratchy tickling at his throat or the steady clack-clack-clack of the rain. He reached up to scratch his throat, finding the blanket had somehow tangled around his neck. He tried to tug it loose, but it seemed bunched up behind his head and resisted.

Then he realized that the clack-clack-clacking he heard was not the rain. Too close, inside the apartment.

He cracked his eyes open then squinted against the white light from the laptop screen. Open not to Instagram, as it had been when he went to sleep, but to a Word document. Bold black text appeared in block rows across the page, the keys depressing with no fingers touching them, causing the clack-clack-clack sound. A ghost writer at work.

Berkley started to rise up, but the blanket around his throat tightened, cutting off his air supply. He clawed at the material, trying to pry his fingers between it and his flesh, but the blanket tightened even more and he felt yanked back, as if someone were pulling from behind. Which was impossible since he was lying flat on the sofa, nothing behind him but cushions.

Of course, he now lived in a place where the impossible was possible.

He gasped for air, finding only a trickle where he needed a gush. He continued to claw at the blanket that had become a noose, his entire body bucking as if he were being electrocuted. His legs kicked out, and one foot caught the edge of the coffee table. The laptop and the bowl of Ramen fell onto the carpeted floor with muffled thuds, but he barely registered this. The only thing that mattered was getting oxygen into his lungs.

He rolled over off the sofa, his knee landing in the cold wet mess of noodles, and began crawling toward the kitchen area. He thought he might have some vague notion of getting a pair of scissors out of the junk drawer or a butcher knife and cutting the blanket off of him, but in truth he operated mainly on instinct.

However, he had barely begun to make progress when the blanket pulled him back. He dug his nails into the nap of the carpet but could not prevent himself from being drug backward. He flipped over onto his back and bent his knees, planting his feet firmly on the floor. This succeeded in stopping the momentum, but did nothing about the blanket strangling him.

It's not the blanket. It's Kevin. He failed at drowning me, so now he's trying to choke me to death.

He raised his head and reached behind his neck, finding the knot in the blanket and picking at it. His vision began to gray at the edges and he wanted to close his eyes and go back to sleep, but then he banged his head against the floor, the pain snapping him back to full consciousness long enough for him to work the knot loose.

As the blanket fell away, he rolled onto his hands and knees and gulped air like a thirsting man might gulp water from a cool spring. His throat felt sore, and he suspected by morning he would have a bruise ringing his neck like a grotesque necklace.

A choker.

He sat up, butt on the floor with his back against the base of the sofa, breathing deeply. Dimly he became aware of the laptop near his right hand. It appeared undamaged from the fall. Not really wanting to know but feeling he had to know, he picked it up and read the message that had been written on the Word document.

```
I can't do this anymore. Just getting
up in the morning hurts. I mean
physically hurts. Every time someone
talks to me it feels like ground glass
in my ears. The sunlight stabs at my
eyes. Breathing is like an anvil
sitting on my chest. I don't think I
was meant to survive Kevin's attack. I
should have gone with him because
there's nothing left for me here. I
know I can't tell you not to be sad or
upset but just know that this is what I
want and I'll be better off dead.
```

A suicide note. Kevin had written a suicide note for Berkley. Would Sasha or Ernie or even Zane have come to check on him, and found him strung up from the ceiling fan and this note on the laptop?

Berkley grabbed his cell phone off the coffee table and quickly called Sasha's number. It was a little after eleven p.m. and he hoped she would still be awake. Three rings, and just as he feared he would get her voicemail, she answered.

"You dodge my calls all day then decide to call me at this hour?" she said without greeting or preamble. "I should tell you to – "

"Can you come over?" Berkley interrupted, his words coming out in a desperate hoarse croak, and the sound of his own pathetic voice caused him to start crying. "Please come over. I need you."

"I'll be right there."

*

They sat on the rickety stools at the bar, because Berkley didn't feel comfortable on either the bed or sofa now. Upon arrival, Sasha had made a pot of coffee – "I doubt either of us will be getting much sleep tonight anyway," she'd reasoned – and poured them both steaming mugs while Berkley recounted the incident with the blanket and read her the "suicide note." Berkley's coffee remained untouched, going lukewarm as he stared into its murky depths. He'd heard of reading tea leaves to divine the future, but what about coffee grounds? He could ask Sasha to dig the muddied filter out of the trash.

"You sure you don't want to leave here?" Sasha asked again. She'd already posed this question a half dozen times, and he knew it was merely a projection of her own desire to leave. But to her credit, she was here and she seemed prepared to stay the night.

"Wouldn't matter," Berkley answered. "I just need someone with me, physically with me, to make sure nothing happens to me."

Left unspoken was the possibility that something could happen to Sasha, but he didn't think it would. Kevin's beef was with Berkley, no one else.

"We could always play a game to pass the time. Not the one we played last time, though."

Berkley laughed at this. "I'm sorry I dragged you out so late. Hope Jeffrey's not too pissed at me."

Berkley knew instantly by the way Sasha began to drum her nails on the bar top that something was wrong; it was her tell. "Well, actually, Jeffrey's staying with his cousin Parker right now."

"Oh," was all Berkley could muster.

"It was a long time coming. You were right about him, I simply couldn't see it. It's for the best, and it has nothing to do with anything going on with you."

Berkley suspected that it had at least a little something to do with him and his situation. Not all, that much was true, but at least a percentage.

"Sorry to hear that. I mean, you can do better, but still … I'm sorry."

"Yeah, breakups are always tough," Sasha said then finished off her coffee.

Unless Jeffrey breaks in and drowns you in the tub, your breakup isn't nearly as tough as my last one.

Sasha began drumming her nails again then said, "I guess Zane should put you in touch with their medium friend after all."

Berkley instinctively reached for his cell and checked it for a message he knew wasn't there. "I've been waiting to hear from Zane, but they haven't been in touch. I haven't heard anything about a medium friend."

"I know, that's my fault. I asked them to hold off telling you."

"Why?"

"I was scared," Sasha said, not quite able to meet his gaze. "It felt like the Ouija board only made things worse. I got worried that having some psychic or whatever in here trying to make contact could potentially amp things up even more."

She clearly feared he would be angry with her, but Berkley was too exhausted for anger. Plus, her concerns were warranted.

"You're right," he said. "May not help, might even hurt. But I have to give it a try. Kevin wants to kill me. This could be my only chance at getting rid of him."

Not exactly, but Berkley hadn't mentioned his meeting with Kevin's sister. He wasn't sure why. Maybe because he had a hunch Sasha would think it was a bad idea, try to talk him out of it or want to tag along as chaperone, which he worried would make Kaitlin clam up.

"I know," Sasha said. "I'll call Zane in the morning."

"You two have gotten awfully chummy lately."

He thought he detected a slight blush. "They're a nice person. Easy to talk to, you know."

Berkley nodded then was overcome by one of those full-body yawns that felt more like a seizure.

"You should try to get some rest," Sasha said.

"No rest for the wicked. Miles to go before I sleep, isn't that the saying?"

"Still, you should try. I'll be here, and I'll stay up to make sure … well, just to make sure."

Berkley settled on the sofa, this time sans blanket, curled up on one end while Sasha sat on the other. She popped her Bluetooth in her ear so that she could watch videos on her phone without the noise disturbing Berkley.

Scrunched up in an almost fetal position, he found himself comforted by her presence and closed his eyes. Yet despite the comfort of having his friend close and the fact that he didn't partake of the caffeine, sleep would not come.

15: Sister

Berkley arrived at Bella Latte half an hour early, taking a seat in the far corner and downing espresso shots like a frat boy with tequila. Last night he had not had any of the coffee, but now he needed the constant jolt of caffeine to keep his brain from atrophying.

Sasha had been up all night as well, and she'd called off from work. Berkley had feared she would want to spend the day with him, but instead she had gone back to her own apartment to crash. She'd asked him to come with her, but he'd said he had errands to run and would meet up with her later. He'd managed a couple hours of broken sleep which provided no real rest.

After ordering his fourth espresso, his phone buzzed. Seeing the name on the Caller ID, he quickly answered.

"Zane, you got good news for me?"

"Well, I've got news anyway."

"Sasha told me you knew someone who might be able to help."

"Yeah, Sasha and I talked earlier this morning."

Again Berkley was struck by the strangeness of Sasha and Zane having their own private friendship apart from him. It felt oddly as if he were being pushed out of his own life, but now was not the time to dwell on that.

"So who's this psychic?" Berkley asked.

"A medium. Psychics can see the future; mediums communicate with the dead."

"Whatever. I'm not interested in the semantics. Can she help me or not?"

"It's a he, guy named Dillard, and he's willing to give it a shot. He's in one of the paranormal Facebook groups where I put out feelers, and he's local. Lives up in

Gaffney. Says if you're available tonight, he can drop by the apartment around seven."

"That's perfect. Do you and Sasha want to come over?"

"Actually, no. I mean, we want to, but Dillard said the fewer people around when he does his thing, the better. Something about too many competing energies jamming his frequencies or something."

For a moment, Berkley wondered if this was all a huge mistake. Dillard sounded like a flake, one of those phony spiritual advisers who used to populate morning talk shows. At most, he'd probably burn some sage and recite a few nonsensical rhyming couplets. The chances of him being the real deal and doing any substantial good were slim.

Then again, slim chances were better than none.

"Fine," he said. "Let's do it."

"Okay. I'll shoot him a message, give him your address."

"Does he need me to provide materials? Candles or incense or anything like that?"

"No, he said he'll bring whatever he needs. He actually seems really intrigued by this whole situation. He said in his experience, true hauntings are extremely rare."

"He hit the jackpot with me then."

"Apparently so," Zane said with a soft laugh. "I told him about what I experienced both at your apartment and the store, gave him the background with Kevin. Definitely has his interest."

"That's good to know. I can't thank you enough for hooking me up with this guy."

"I only hope it helps. Sasha and I agreed to hang out at her apartment tonight, so you call us as soon as Dillard leaves. Let us know how it all pans out."

"Will do, my friend. And thanks again."

After ending the call and finishing his fourth espresso, Berkley switched to plain coffee. Black. He'd gotten through half the mug when Kaitlin Sparks walked into the shop.

He knew it was her instantly, and not simply from the way she scanned the place as if looking for someone. In her features, he could clearly see shades of Kevin. The prominent cheekbones, the eyebrows that made almost perfect natural peaks, the slightly too-wide eyes lending an appearance of perpetual surprise.

Raising a hand, he waved Kaitlin over. She approached slowly, a wariness in her step. "You must be Berkley," she said when she reached the table.

"Yes. Have a seat, please."

She hesitated, continuing to glance around as if scoping out the closest escape routes. Finally she sat across from Berkley and held out a hand. "Nice to meet you, though under the circumstances that might sound like an inappropriate thing to say."

Berkley shook the proffered hand, noting how his own shook with slight tremors. Mostly from the overdose of caffeine, but at least part of it had to do with the resemblance to Kevin. In some ways, he felt as if he were staring into the face of a reincarnation.

"You look like him," he blurted.

Kaitlin's only answer was a grimace.

"Would you like a drink?" Berkley asked.

"No, I really can't stay long. I just … well, after what my brother put you through, I guess I felt like I owed you something."

"Not your fault, but I do have some questions. Stan

hinted about some stuff from Kevin's childhood. Both your childhoods, I guess. I want to know about it."

"Why?" Kaitlin asked with another grimace. "I mean, do you really think it will help?"

"Honestly, I don't know, but he did try to kill me. I want to at least make an attempt to understand why, what might have led him to that kind of behavior."

She considered it for a moment then blew out her breath in a long sigh. "It's nothing all that extraordinary. Merely your run of the mill dysfunctional family trauma. That's much more typical and all-American than that idealized, bubblegum *Leave it to Beaver* and *Brady Bunch* bullshit. Of course, it didn't start out bad, at least not on the surface. To me and Kevin, things seemed fine and normal until the day our mother left."

"How old were the two of you?"

"Let see … I was six so that would have made Kevin eight. Lots of kids have parents who divorce, but the really messed up thing was how my mother went about it. It was sometime in the summer, so Kevin and I were out of school. She waited until our father went to work then she sat the two of us down and told us that she wasn't cut out for this wife and mommy business. She had us young and hadn't really finished growing up herself. She said she had to go have some fun, experience life, and she couldn't do that tied down with a family. She explained that she couldn't love us the way a mother should love her children. She actually said that to us. Then she told us she'd left cereal out on the kitchen table if we got hungry, went upstairs and packed a bag, and left. She left us alone, an eight year old and a six year old. We didn't know what to do, and we didn't even know our father's work number. We simply waited around the house, eating Fruity Pebbles and watching TV until our father got home after five that evening."

"That's horrible," Berkley said and meant it. "Did you ever see your mother again?"

Kaitlin shook her head. "I don't think our father tried very hard to find her, and he got divorce papers served a year later. She didn't ask for anything, and he signed them. She never called or even sent a card. She simply disappeared from our lives."

This explained a lot about Kevin's abandonment issues. Didn't cause Berkley to feel sympathy for the man exactly, but it at least shed some light on his motivations, twisted as they might have been.

"How did your father react to her leaving?" Berkley asked, sensing there was yet more to the story.

"He withdrew. Frankly, he was never the warmest of fathers. Distant, not particularly affectionate, but after our mother left, Kevin and I became practically invisible to him. Even at so young, we had to learn to fend for ourselves. Got ourselves up and dressed in the mornings, made our own meals. Mostly consisting of cereal and sandwiches and lots of chocolate. Whole days would pass without our father even speaking to us or acknowledging us. He didn't pay us the slightest attention unless … "

"Unless what?" Berkley prompted. He could tell by the woman's posture, expression, and tone that this was painful for her, a subject she'd rather not discuss, but he had to know.

Knowledge is power!

After a moment to steel herself, Kaitlin went on. "We discovered that if we did something to really annoy our father, be it making too much noise or breaking something or spilling chocolate milk on the carpet, he would notice us then and give us some rather violent attention. And I'm not talking normal spankings, but real beatings. The kind that left bruises and welts and on occasion black eyes. After the first couple of times it happened to me, I learned to stay out of my father's way, but Kevin's reaction was the extreme opposite. He seemed to thrive on antagonizing our father, as if he considered that kind of violent attention better than neglect. I swear, he went out of his way to purposefully provoke our father and the beatings seemed to make him happy in a perverse way. Almost like they were proof our father loved him, or at least noticed him which Kevin perhaps considered a suitable substitute for love."

More puzzle pieces snapping into place, the picture becoming clearer. No less disturbing, but at least clearer.

"Once I hit my teens, I started spending as much time out of the house as possible, staying with friends. Our father died when I was eighteen and Kevin twenty. I didn't attend the funeral, not sure if Kevin did or not. By that point, we weren't talking much. Over the years, I tried to reconnect with my brother, but for reasons I guess I'll never know he didn't seem to have much interest."

"Did you go to *his* funeral?"

Kaitlin nodded. "I know what our parents did to us really warped Kevin, but I still remember the boy he was. Hurt and lost … and broken. Turns out irreparably. I planned and paid for the funeral, not so much for the man he'd become but for the boy he'd been."

Berkley felt as if he could cry. For Kevin, for himself, even for this woman sitting across from him whom he barely knew. Was this perhaps the key to everything? Understanding and empathy? How could he use that?

"I'm not making excuses for my brother," Kaitlin

said. "What he did to you is unforgivable. However, I don't believe Kevin had a truly contented moment his entire life, living a miserable existence. At the very least, I hope now he's found some kind of peace."

Before Berkley could respond to that, his coffee mug slid off the side of the table and shattered on the tiled floor.

16: The Medium

Berkley checked the time again. 6:37 p.m. So one minute later than the last time he'd checked.

He couldn't be still. He would sit for a few seconds then hop back up and begin pacing around the apartment. Periodically the water in the kitchen sink or bathroom tub would turn on but he would simply ignore it until it went off again. The TV turned itself on at one point, the volume turning up to ear-shattering decibels before flipping off again.

Berkley stepped into the kitchen area, taking a rag and wiping down the counter despite the fact that he'd already done this a half dozen times. He'd straightened up the entire apartment, in fact. One full cleaning, and then a lot of maintenance as books fell from the bookcase and had to be returned to the shelves. A part of him found it strange how quickly this sort of thing no longer seemed strange, merely a commonplace aspect of his life, but he didn't dwell. Instead too focused on the clock and the immediate arrival of the psychic. Correction, *medium*.

For the first time since all this insanity began, Berkley had a clear plan and he was eager to put it into motion. It wasn't the most elaborate of plans, but he thought it had a shot at working. He really did think understanding and empathy were the twin keys. The picture Kaitlin painted of her brother was that of a tragic figure, whose past of abandonment and neglect and abuse had irrevocably twisted him. Not so much a monster as a victim of his own misfortune.

Not that Berkley didn't hold Kevin responsible for his own actions. Plenty of people have shitty childhoods, many worse than Kevin's, and manage to overcome the past to evolve into functioning and productive adults. Sasha was a prime example of this. But knowing the contributing factors behind Kevin's nature opened a doorway of compassion that Berkley hoped he could exploit to put an end to the haunting. He simply needed to be able to communicate directly with Kevin. One on one, man to man.

Which was where Dillard came in.

A light tapping at 6:42 sent Berkley bounding to the door, flinging it open only to be disappointed when he found Ernie standing outside.

"What do you want?" he asked more curtly than he'd intended.

Ernie looked sheepish in the waning evening light, hands stuffed deep in his pockets. "I hadn't heard from you so I just wanted to check in. Make sure you're okay."

"I'm fine, but I can't talk right now. I'm expecting company. He'll be here soon."

"Oh, *he*. Okay, I understand. I don't want to interrupt a hot date or anything."

"It's not like that," Berkley said with an exasperated sigh. "It's a medium that Zane hooked me up with. The guy's going to help me communicate with Kevin and hopefully get rid of him."

The relief on Ernie's face would have been endearing if it hadn't been so nakedly desperate. "That's great, Berk. You want me to stick around, join in the séance or whatever?"

"No, Ernie. Can't jam his frequencies, apparently."

Berkley waited for Ernie to go back over to his own apartment, but instead he continued to stand there. Finally he said, "I want to apologize for the other night. If I did something wrong – "

"It wasn't you," Berkley interrupted. "I'm the one who should be saying sorry. It's a weird time for me right now, and I'm not acting myself. I didn't mean to hurt your feelings."

"That's okay. I mean, it's understandable."

"Then we're cool?"

Ernie smiled. "Of course we are."

"Glad to hear it. Now I really need to finish getting ready before the medium gets here."

"I won't keep you. Let me know how it goes."

Before Ernie had even finished speaking, Berkley was already closing the door in his face. He knew he should feel at least a little bad for the way he was treating his neighbor, but Berkley had problems much bigger than some Bear's doomed crush.

The next knock came at 6:53, and when Berkley opened the door this time he found a stranger waiting. Surely the medium though not at all what Berkley had been expecting. He couldn't say exactly what he had been expecting, but this wasn't it.

For one, the guy was young. From his appearance, Berkley would guess fresh out of high school. He was dressed casually in jeans and a Siouxsie and the Banshees T. His nails were painted black, and his matching hair done up in a high pompadour style. He seemed the quintessential "too cool for school" type.

Yet the most bizarre thing about him was what he carried with him. A tall, thin mirror, the kind someone might hang on the back of a closet door.

"Dillard?" Berkley said skeptically.

The young man smiled. "In the corporeal flesh. You can call me Tangina."

"What?"

"Sorry, just a little occupational humor. Can I come in?"

Bemused, Berkley stepped aside and allowed Dillard to enter. The young man leaned the mirror against the wall just inside the door then began to mill about the apartment, nodding and mumbling to himself. When the circuit brought him back around to the bathroom, he reached in and flipped on the light.

"Product of your mischievous phantom?" Dillard asked.

Berkley walked over to find the bathroom floor once again wet. With a weary dip of his chin, he nodded.

Dillard began walking around the apartment again, this time stopping in the very center with his hands on his hips. "The air in here is heavy, man. Like the heaviest I've ever felt. It's like trying to walk underwater."

Berkley leaned against the bathroom doorjamb, starting to fear tonight was going to be a bust. This young man whose youthful confidence seemed almost unnatural, carrying around his own full-sized mirror as if he couldn't stand to not look at himself when on the go … Berkley found it hard to believe Dillard would be able to help him.

"So," Berkley said, just to make conversation, "Zane tells me that you believe true hauntings are rare."

"Most definitely. Despite what the movies would have you think, when a spirit departs a body, it doesn't hang around. It moves on to the next plane, eager for the next leg of the journey."

"Next plane?" Berkley repeated. "You mean Heaven?"

Dillard shrugged. "I don't know much about what comes after. That isn't for the living to know. Call it what you will, be it Heaven or Paradise or the Elysian Fields, it's where spirits go when they've shed the mortal trappings of flesh. When I do my work, I have to actually call them back to this plane, which takes some effort, because wherever they are, they aren't here."

"So all the stories you hear about haunted houses and such are made up?"

"Not all. There are a few instances of spirits getting stuck here on this plane after death, although most legit cases are poltergeist activity."

"Poltergeist," Berkley said softly. "Like that movie. Oh, Tangina, now I get it."

"Good flick, original anyway," Dillard said, "but it gets the concept of the poltergeist all wrong. A poltergeist isn't a haunting at all. It is the result of latent telekinetic abilities. Some living person is causing all the events unconsciously, totally unaware, and attributes it to a spirit."

"So you think I'm causing all this with my mind or something?"

"Doubtful. Most poltergeist incidents involve adolescents, because that is a time of life when hormones are raging combined with physiological changes which lead to a kind of stress that makes them feel helpless and not in control of their own bodies. It's that precise mix of ingredients that make the situation ripe for poltergeist activity."

Berkley found himself reevaluating his initial opinion of Dillard. The young man certainly seemed to know what he was talking about, and his confidence was actually inspiring and infectious.

"Besides," Dillard said, "I can feel the presence of an energy in this place that isn't yours or mine. Rare as it is, you've got yourself a genuine haunting, my friend."

It felt perverse, but hearing Dillard say that actually triggered a relief response. Sort of like a diagnosis of cancer can seem like a blessing after months of not knowing what was wrong with you. Once the exact problem has been identified then a treatment plan can be put into place.

"How did you get into this kind of work?" Berkley asked.

"I wouldn't call it work, exactly. I don't get paid for it. It's just a natural talent. A gift some might say. Discovered I had the ability when I was ten. My grandmother had passed away, and my mother's grief was all-consuming. I remember one night I was in the bathroom, standing on my little stool and brushing my teeth at the sink, wishing that my mother could talk to my grandmother at least one more time. Then I felt kind of faint and blacked out. When I came back to myself, I was still standing on the stool, but my mother was in the room, sitting on the edge of the tub and crying. She said she walked into the bathroom to see what was taking me so long, and saw me standing in front of the mirror. Except the reflection wasn't me, but my grandmother. When I started to talk to her, it wasn't my voice she heard, but my grandmother's. They talked, my grandmother assured her she was safe and warm and happy where she was. Brought a lot of peace to my mother."

Berkley glanced at the mirror resting beside the door, thinking he was beginning to understand its significance and purpose. "Do you think you'll be able to get Kevin to talk to me?"

"I've never failed to call a spirit," Dillard said with more of that casual, easy confidence.

"When do we start?"

"No time like the present."

Dillard walked over to the bar and grabbed two of the stools, carrying them across the apartment and placing them about six feet apart. Then he retrieved his mirror and propped it up on top of Berkley's low dresser. The young man settled himself on the stool closest to the mirror, the other stool straight back from him.

"Okay," Dillard said. "You sit on the stool behind me. Once I go into my trance, you'll no longer see my reflection in the mirror. Instead, you'll see the image of the spirit. When I speak, it will be with the spirit's voice. It can be disconcerting, which is why I'm warning you beforehand."

Berkley sat on his stool, staring over Dillard's shoulder at their doubles in the mirror. "This will really work?"

"I'd offer you a money-back-guarantee, but you aren't paying me anything. Tell you what, if this doesn't work, I'll give you twenty bucks."

Berkley knew this was meant as a joke, but he didn't have it in him to laugh. In the mirror, he saw Dillard close his eyes and his face went slack, all the facial muscles relaxing. He looked even younger.

This is so stupid. The young man might talk a good game, but he's a fraud just like every palm reader with those tacky signs on the highway. Okay, so he isn't trying to scam me out of money like they are, which just means he's more than likely got a few screws loose in his noggin.

Berkley's eyes had dropped to his lap, but when he looked back up and into the mirror, what he saw there made him gasp.

17: Empty

Dillard came back to himself with a shudder. He blinked several times, shook his head, then rubbed at the back of his neck.

"How long was I out?" Dillard asked, his words fuzzy around the edges like someone just waking from a long deep sleep. He checked his watch. "Ten minutes, huh? Not the longest I've ever been out. So how did it go? Did you get what you needed out of the encounter?"

Berkley sat still for a moment before answering, his face reflecting back to him from the mirror a perfect blank. "There was no encounter. Nothing happened."

Dillard turned quickly on his stool so that the two men faced each other. "What do you mean, nothing happened?"

"Just that. You sat there with your eyes closed for ten minutes, and I waited for something to happen. Nothing did."

The young man laughed as if he thought Berkley were making a tasteless joke, but his eyes were wounded and perhaps a bit offended. "No way. I've never failed to call a spirit. And this one seemed particularly eager to communicate."

"I don't know what to tell you. Maybe the spirit is playing games with us, or maybe I'm just crazy after all."

Dillard shook his head vigorously. "There's a spiritual presence in this apartment. I can still feel it. Let's try again."

Berkley stood. "Really, it's not a big deal. You gave it your best shot. Kevin's being tight-lipped, that's all. If he doesn't want to talk, we can't make him."

"The hell I can't," Dillard said, spinning to face the mirror again. "Just give me a couple of minutes to get back in the right head space and we'll do this thing."

Berkley walked over to the young man and gently took his arm. "I think you should go. I'm feeling a bit worn out."

Getting to his feet, Dillard stared intensely at Berkley. "Are you sure nothing happened? You look a little … *off*. Shaken up."

"Can you blame me? This has been a nightmare for me, and I pinned all my hopes on you and then to have it all turn out to be a big bust is a little disheartening, to say the least."

"Man, I'm so sorry. I don't know why it didn't work."

"I'm not blaming you," Berkley said softly, letting the young man retrieve his mirror then leading him toward the door. "Maybe we'll try it again another night, but right now I need some alone time."

At the door, Dillard paused, dug his wallet out of pocket, and offered a twenty. "I did promise."

Berkley pushed the money away. "Don't be ridiculous. You did your best. This pesky spirit is simply … unpredictable."

"I'm going to be in touch. My pride is on the line here, and I will make this spirit talk if I have to grab him by the tongue and force the words out of him."

"Nice imagery," Berkley said with a wan smile. "You drive safe, and have a good night."

After he shuffled Dillard out of the apartment, Berkley stood for a moment with his back against the door. Like the medium, Berkley too could sense the presence in the apartment. Hovering, watching, waiting, full of anticipation. Only one thing would appease this spirit and put an end to this emptiness that had become Berkley's existence, he knew that now.

There was only one course of action, but there was a little something he had to do first. Just to ensure he would not be interrupted.

Berkley called Sasha, who answered on the first ring. "So what happened? Problem solved?"

"It was very productive."

"Productive? We're not talking about a business meeting. What does that mean?"

Berkley chose his next words carefully. "I would say mission accomplished. After tonight I'm confident there will be no more spiritual disturbances. I'm finally going to have some peace and quiet."

A beat of silence from the other end then Sasha said, her voice tentative with cautious hope, "Really? It's over? It can't be that simple."

"I didn't say it was simple. I had a conversation I didn't want to have but I needed to have."

"But … wait a minute, hold on. Zane says they just got a message from Dillard, and according to Dillard it didn't work."

Damn it, should have known the medium would be in contact with Zane.

"I know, that's what I told him."

"Why?"

"Because what transpired was deeply personal. I don't actually know Dillard and didn't feel comfortable getting into it with him. Figured it would be best to tell him nothing happened."

"What about me? You know, your best friend since forever. Do you feel comfortable telling me what really happened?"

"I will," Berkley said, his first outright lie. "But

tomorrow. The whole thing left me feeling very drained, mentally and emotionally and even physically. I want to sleep and then tomorrow morning I'll give you all the details."

"Zane and I can come over if you don't want to be alone."

"Thank you, but no. For the first time since I got back from the hospital, I'm not worried about being alone. In fact, I'm looking forward to it."

Another beat of silence. "Are you sure?"

"Positive. Maybe we can meet up in the morning. You, me, and Zane. Get donuts at Krispy Kreme or something."

"Seven?"

"Sounds good. And Sasha?"

"Yes."

Berkley held the phone away from his face for a few seconds as he fought to keep his emotions in check. He didn't want Sasha to hear a tremor in his voice that might give him away. Finally, after a deep breath, he said, "I want to thank you. For everything. You really are the best friend a guy could have. I wouldn't have been able to get through all this craziness without you."

"Getting you through craziness is in my job description," she chided, though he thought he detected emotion causing her voice to quaver.

"Maybe, but I think dealing with a ghost goes above and beyond. You're due for some overtime and hazard pay."

"Want me to call you in the morning or just meet you at Krispy Kreme?"

"You can call."

"Okay, honey. I hope that you manage to get some

sleep."

"I think I'll finally be able to sleep. Tell Zane thanks as well."

"You got it."

After hanging up, Berkley tossed his phone onto the bed. Sasha would call in the morning, but he wouldn't answer.

Going into the bathroom, he sat on the edge of the tub, stoppered the drain then turned on the water, testing the temperature to make sure Goldilocks would approve. He considered leaving a note for Sasha, but in the end he thought their phone conversation would suffice as an appropriate goodbye. It would have to do, in any case.

When the tub was halfway full, Berkley climbed inside, not bothering to undress. He hadn't actually been in the tub for anything other than a shower, not actually sitting and submerging in the water this way, since the night Kevin had broken in.

But he now realized he'd always been destined to find himself back here again.

Berkley felt tears began to trickle down his face, tickling his cheeks, as the water climbed higher up the tub. He closed his eyes and leaned his head back.

18: Your Own Worst Enemy

When Berkley looked back up and into the mirror, what he saw there made him gasp.

Two men, sitting on stools, one in front of the other. Yet though Berkley could see Dillard's jet-black pompadour just ahead, in the mirror it was not the medium's reflection he saw. Instead, he saw himself. Twice. Once where it should have been, but in Dillard's place in the glass was a duplicate version of Berkley.

"Surprise," the duplicate said, and even though Berkley knew the words were coming from Dillard's mouth, it was his own voice he heard.

"What's going on?" Berkley asked, his voice carrying an almost angry bite. "What kind of trick is this? Where's Kevin?"

In the mirror, the duplicate smiled. "Kevin's gone. You heard our trendy little medium here. Usually when someone dies, their spirit skedaddles on to the higher plane or wherever. Same with Kevin. The second that bullet passed through his cerebral cortex, his soul vamoosed out of here."

"No, that's not possible. This apartment is haunted."

"Well, technically it's you that's haunted, not the apartment, but you already know that. What you don't know is that you're haunting yourself."

"So it is a poltergeist thing?" Berkley asked. "This is all in my mind?"

The duplicate shook his head. "Afraid not. The haunting is very much real."

"I can't be the ghost. I'm not dead."

"No, you're not. This isn't some Sixth Sense bullshit. And that's the crux of the problem."

Berkley began tugging at his hair, a headache forming just behind his eyes. "What are you talking about? I don't understand."

"Your lack of understanding is understandable. This is a complicated situation, but I'll try to lay it out as clearly as possible, because it is important that you understand. So that you can do what you have to do. For starters, you did die. You drowned, and you were dead."

"But Ernie resuscitated me."

The duplicate sighed. "And that's what caused this whole mess. Poor Ernie, he meant well. He couldn't know he was screwing everything up."

"Screwing things up how?*"*

"I won't pretend I know all the rules, if there is some kind of time threshold or not, but I do know that you were dead just long enough for your spirit, your soul, to detach from your body. That's me, buddy. And when your body was revived, I didn't join back up. I'm a separate entity now. And yet I am tethered to the body, like some kind of spiritual umbilical cord, so that next plane Dillard talked about, I can't move on to it. As long as the body I'm tethered to still lives, I'm trapped here. And that is exactly how it feels, like I'm trapped. I feel this call, this pull, to the other side, but every time I try to make that jump, I get yanked back because of the leash I'm on."

"This is insane. How can I be walking around and breathing if I have no soul?"

The duplicate tilted his head, his expression one of pity. "I know you feel it. The emptiness inside. You are walking around and breathing, but isn't that all you're doing? Not living, that's for sure. Ever since you woke up in that hospital, you've felt my absence. You have no emotional connection with the people in your life, you find no enjoyment in anything. That's because you can't; you don't the capability without me. You told that shrink you felt like a zombie, and in a lot of ways you were closer to the truth in that statement than you realized when you said it. Your body is living, but you're dead on the inside where it counts the most."

Berkley started to protest again, but then paused. So much of what the duplicate said made sense. It was insane, but the situation itself was insane and the duplicate's reasoning actually explained a lot about why he felt so hollow.

"Can't I ever get any better, get my spark back?" he asked.

That pitying look from the duplicate again. "There is no you, not really. I'm the real *Berkley Simmons. The one who loves to dance, who harbors a secret dream of doing musical theater, who finds inspiration from the view at the top of the Raven Cliff's hiking trail. You're only a shell, and that's all you'll ever be. You can take the shrink's advice and go through the motions from now until Doom's Day, but no, you'll never get your spark back because I'm the spark and I'm done with the flesh. I want to move on from here, I need to, and I simply can't wait around in this limbo another fifty years for you to kick the bucket from old age."*

"You've been doing all this to me to ... what? Goad me into killing myself?"

"I didn't know what else to do. It's the only solution."

Berkley glanced over at the sofa. "You tried to kill me last night."

The duplicate shrugged casually, as if accused of nothing more serious than double parking. "The longer I'm stuck here, the stronger I get and the more I figure out what I'm capable of. And I will continue this campaign against you for as long as it takes, years if need be. Hell, I've got nothing if not time. Nothing personal, just self-preservation. Ask yourself, is it really worth it for you to fight me? For a life you don't even feel an attachment to in the first place? What are you fighting for exactly? Another several decades of drifting along and feeling nothing for anything or anyone? Doesn't sound like much of a prize, does it?"

"I'm scared," Berkley said, wrapping his arms around himself.

"I know, but the hard part's already over. Death is actually a natural part of existence. What's happening now, that's what is unnatural. You need to let go so that Berkley Simmons can undertake that next mysterious journey. You need to give up the ghost ... literally."

Berkley and his duplicate shared a soft chuckle over that one, and then he realized that he had perhaps been looking at this wrong. Maybe he was the duplicate. He sat for a moment, contemplating all he'd learned, trying to sort through everything in his mind, rearranging all the bits and pieces of information in an attempt to get a cohesive picture.

"Are you sure?" Berkley asked. "That you can't, you know, get back in, merge, whatever?"

"I'm positive. Right after the separation, I tried repeatedly. No dice. Fact is, you don't have a soul. You shouldn't still be alive, and until that is rectified, we're both screwed. You have the answer that will solve this problem, the capacity to free us both from our misery. Seems like a no-brainer to me. I mean, when you get right down to it, what are you living for?"

2B

Berkley stared down at his lap again, trying to formulate a response to that question and coming up empty. When he raised his head, he was surprised to see there were no longer dual reflections of himself in the mirror. There was him and there was the medium.

Another minute played out in a pregnant silence, and then Dillard came back to himself with a shudder.

Epilogue: Goodbyes

Sasha stood by the grave, staring silently at the marker with the name Berkley Andrew Simmons engraved into the stone. Zane stood next to her.

Sasha had visited the grave every single day for the month since the funeral, usually stopping by after work during the week and mid-mornings on the weekends. And Zane had accompanied her for each trip. She had assured them that they didn't have to, but they insisted. That was just the kind of person they were.

Thunder rumbled in the distance, but not terribly distant, suggesting rather pointedly she should keep this visit brief. Still she lingered.

"I can't get over how Berkley's brother acted during the funeral," she said, rehashing a favorite sore subject for her. "Like it was all nothing but a terrible inconvenience for him. Not even a trace of grief, only this sense that this was a chore he would rather not be doing. It was disgraceful."

Zane did the one-shoulder shrug. "At least he showed up. When I go, I'm sure none of my family will bother. They pretty much disowned me when I came out as non-binary, and if they do talk to me, they seem to go out of their way to mis-gender me."

Sasha leaned to the left, resting her head on Zane's shoulder. "I'm sorry. I know I'm going on, but I'm so damn angry. Mostly I'm angry with myself."

Zane took her hand. "None of this is your fault. There's nothing you could have done."

"I should have gone over there that night after talking to him on the phone. I should have sensed something was wrong."

"I was there with you," Zane reminded, "and I had

no inkling of what he was planning either."

Sasha felt tears threaten, and she granted herself the freedom to let them flow. "Should have been a red flag when he lied to Dillard and said the attempt to contact Kevin didn't work."

"Maybe it didn't," Zane said. "Maybe the lie he told was to us. Think about it, what if he put all his eggs into Dillard's basket? If it didn't work then maybe he felt he had no other recourse."

Sasha sniffled and swiped at her leaking eyes. "You think that could be it?"

"I don't know, and since he didn't leave a note, we'll never really know."

"It's possible he didn't kill himself at all," Sasha said, giving voice to a fear she'd harbored since finding out about Berkley. She didn't want to face it, but it had to be faced. "It could have been like what happened to him the night before with the blanket wrapping around his throat. Kevin could have done it and made it look like a suicide."

"You're right, that's at least possible, but again we'll never really know."

Sasha wished she could accept such ambiguity, but it simply wasn't in her nature. She didn't even like books or movies that had open endings, loose ends, unresolved plot threads. They actually made her angry. She needed definitive closure, preferably with an epilogue that let her know what happened to each of the characters after the story ended.

"Have you talked to Ernie lately?" Zane asked.

"He's still a wreck. Absolutely heartbroken and inconsolable. I don't know what to do for him."

"He shouldn't be alone. Let's invite him out to a movie or to go bowling or something. Anything to get him out of self-isolation."

Sasha turned to Zane and smiled through her tears. "You're pretty amazing, you know that?"

"I do what I can."

Thunder grumbled loud and long, and lightning flashed purple through the gathering clouds.

"Let's go before Zeus throws a bolt at us," Zane said.

Sasha didn't want to go, but she allowed Zane to lead her back through the Greenlawn Cemetery to where they had left the car. She knew she would be back tomorrow, and though she hadn't verbalized it, she also knew why she kept coming back.

She wanted to feel a presence, receive some kind of a sign. If Kevin could linger after his death, why not Berkley? Maybe he would try to communicate, let her know he was okay. So far no such luck.

At the car, she paused before getting in, her eyes staring across the expanse and immediately zeroing in on Berkley's marker. Despite the static-electricity of the imminent storm crackling in the air, at the gravesite nothing moved.

All was still.

THE END

2B

About the Author

Mark Allan Gunnells loves to tell stories. He has since he was a kid, penning one-page tales that were Twilight Zone knockoffs. He likes to think he has gotten a little better since then. He loves reader feedback, and above all he loves telling stories. He lives in Greer, SC, with his husband Craig A. Metcalf. https://amzn.to/2JctkEi

About the Publisher

Photo credit: Molly Hayden

Adam Messer is an author, journalist and radio host. He enjoys connecting with other creative people. He is a columnist for the Savannah Morning News Do Savannah. He hosts his radio show The Adam Messer Show live on WRUU 107.5 FM Savannah where he interviews authors, artists, and entertainers. He is the publisher of Valhalla Books, and publishes compelling fiction so that people enjoy reading again. Messer enjoys spending time with his family.

www.adammesser.net

Thank you!

We hope you enjoyed *2B by Mark Allan Gunnells*
We love reader reviews and appreciate your review on
Amazon and/or Goodreads.

Valhalla Books Catalogue:
www.valhallabooks.com/catalogue

The Devil's Due: Nothing Is Ever As It Seems dark spec
fiction anthology. Nothing is ever as it seems. Ill-begotten
wealth, fame, and glory come at a high price.
Featuring award winning authors and Horror Writers
Association members, The Devil's Due offers enthralling
horror stories of underhanded deals gone awry.
https://amzn.to/36CDWDp

2B by **Mark Allan Gunnells -** "When your ex wants you
dead, they will take you to the grave with them!" -2 B

"Berkley Simmons died … for five minutes.

Berkley woke up to find himself in the hospital. He
discovered that his ex is dead after a failed murder/ suicide
attempt. With nowhere else to go, Berkley must return to
the apartment where it all happened.It doesn't take long for
Berkley to begin to suspect that his ex never left the
apartment, and still wants him dead."

Sign up for exclusive inside looks of Valhalla Books at our
newsletter. www.valhallabooks.com

Made in the USA
Middletown, DE
04 September 2021